DOUBLE IMAGE

Also by Pat Moon

The Spying Game

DOUBLE IMAGE

PAT MOON

ORCHARD BOOKS
96 Leonard Street, London EC2A 4RH
Orchard Books Australia
14 Mars Road, Lane Cove, NSW 2066
First published in Great Britain 1993
First paperback publication 1993

A CIP catalogue record for this book is available from the British Library
Paperback 1 85213 761 4
Hardback 1 85213 496 8
Printed at Guernsey Press, C.I.

With thanks to
Rosemary Sandberg

Chapter One

The tiny screwed-paper ball skidded across David's open book. Kelly, sitting next to him, gave a sideways, inquisitive look as David smoothly covered it with one hand, whilst checking with a quick glance that Mr Jones had not noticed. It was ERIC Time, Everybody Reading In Class, which was supposed to include Mr Jones too, though Mark, who sat closer, regularly reported seeing him filling in his football coupon or doing his newspaper crossword.

David's fingers carefully unfolded the ball, out of sight, beneath his desk. This method of communication was an invention of which he was proud. He had discovered it was quite possible to write on paper tissue, so long as you used a handwriting pen and printed large enough to compensate for the slight blurring. Screwed up tightly, the soft tissue ball landed with barely a sound and could be opened silently in class. He and Mark had been using this method for a year now and had not been caught once.

He read the message:

ADD WATERPROOF MATCHES TO THE LIST
MEET AFTER SCHOOL

David pulled his left ear twice to indicate to Mark that the message had been received and understood.

What else did they still need? A tin opener, batteries for the torch, food supplies, fuel, a frying pan . . .

RRRIIIIIING! The shrilling of the school bell crashed into his thoughts. The class stirred from its silent vigil, chairs were scraped back noisily from tables, books slammed shut, and children yawned and stretched their limbs.

Mr Jones looked up, waited for silence, and dismissed them table by table with a nod of his head. David's table was last. As he lifted his chair onto his desk he saw that Mr Jones was already deeply absorbed in studying a colour spread of a golden, palm-treed beach, labelled SUNSEEKERS' PARADISE.

As David reached the cloakroom, the loud voice of Warren Biggs bellowed above the hub-bub of children crowding through the corridor, "I can get waterproof matches and loads of other stuff: groundsheets, ropes, you name it. I only have to ask my dad. No problem."

David saw his friend Mark shrug. "Yeh, well thanks, Warren, but it's a survival thing really, just me and Martian. We've been planning it for weeks."

Everyone in school knew David Marsh as Martian. It had started in the Infants and the name had stuck. He preferred it to David, it made him feel special and seemed particularly suitable for someone like himself with an interest in space exploration. Even Mr Jones had been known to use it. Last term when Jamie Cook had been doing his project and couldn't discover when the first space probe had landed on Mars, Mr Jones had said, "You'd better ask the Martian," and David had instantly responded with, "Viking 1, June 1976. First pictures received June 26th."

The astonished expressions of the rest of the class still gave him a warm glow whenever he thought of it, though he'd since learned to check his enthusiasm for demonstrating his instant recall of facts and figures. He'd seen the warning signs when he'd noticed Paul Harris on the other side of the classroom massaging the air above his head to indicate a large swelling.

Mark shot David a desperate 'come-and-get-me-out-of-this' look. David reached between them and lifted his bag from his peg.

"Mark's just been telling me all about your camp," said Warren. "I could give you a hand. Get some gear from the shop – high-protein food, survival aids, anything you like. How about it?"

"It's not that type of camp," said David. "We're building our own shelter, see, from branches and such like. Anyway, Mark's dad said only two of us. Right, Mark?"

"Yeh, right," nodded Mark eagerly.

"Well, you just think about," said Warren. "It could be worth your while."

They watched him bulldoze his way through the cloakroom, aiming his bulging hold-all before him like a battering ram.

"What did you tell him about the camp for?" accused David as they crossed the playground.

"You're joking!" said Mark. "You think I'd tell

him? He saw me write the note and then he kind of wheedled it out of me. You know what he's like."

"That's why we don't want him. Clear? It'll be the treehouse story all over again. Mr Know-it-all who blames everyone else when things go wrong. This is our project, right?"

"Yes, but that stuff from his dad's camping shop could be pretty useful," said Mark.

"Don't even think about it," said David.

They'd been planning the camp since half-term and, with the summer holiday just a few weeks away, the preparations took up all their spare time.

Mark's large garden backed onto the woods. It was difficult to tell where the two merged as the wire fence that separated them had become buried in brackens and shrubs and the woods had encroached into the garden itself. Unlike David's small, neat garden, you could imagine you were in a wilderness, not just a few minutes away from the lines of traffic that queued in and out of Bromley.

Mark's parents had given them permission to build the camp on the condition they did it safely. Since then, they'd read all the survival books they could find and the project had taken them over. Mark's bedroom walls were covered in plans and drawings and lists. The growing pile of materials and equipment had long since been banished to the shed by Mark's mum.

"How's the fuel supply going?" asked David.

"The wood we collected last week's dried out now," said Mark. "We ought to put it under polythene in case it rains. And there's loads more fallen branches and cones in the woods."

"Right, we'll make another collection tonight," said David. "And on Saturday we'll build a trench-fire and practise cooking some food. I found an old grill-pan in the garage and Mum says we can have it. The wire rack's just perfect for cooking on over the fire."

They separated at the corner of Westlands Road.

"I'll be round as soon as I've changed," shouted David.

He could picture it all so easily: the two of them crouched over a glowing fire, the pan sizzling with sausages and eggs. They'd decide tonight what they'd need and make a list.

It wasn't till he reached his gate that he noticed Eva's purple Mini parked outside. He never called her Gran or Nan. Everyone called her Eva: Mum, Dad, even his little sister, Lizzie. Dad said it wasn't her real name at all. She'd been christened Brenda, but when she and his father had divorced, she'd announced to everyone that she was starting a new life and from then on wished to be known only as Eva.

She wasn't like any other grans he knew and certainly not like Mum's mother, Nan Robinson. He could only vaguely recall her as a gloomy, bad-tempered, occasional visitor who had long ceased visiting them. He had fonder memories of Grandad Robinson though. He could remember bouncing on Grandad's knee to a rhyme that ended with 'and down into the ditch', and David would go plunging between

Grandad's knees to be caught just in time by his large hands, before he hit the floor. They'd both laugh and David would plead, "Again, Grandad, into the ditch again Grandad." But Nan Robinson never laughed. Ever. Just sat there staring coldly into the distance. He hadn't seen them for years now. Only Mum ever saw them now, always on her own, when she'd leave Dad or Eva in charge for a day or two and go down to Wimborne in Dorset, where they lived. But she was always in such a bad mood when she returned that David had come to resent the visits.

There'd been rows too, between Mum and Dad about it. They'd shut the door on him, but it hadn't smothered the raised voices, especially Dad's shouting, "I can't let you do this! She's not going to ruin our family too."

David pushed open the side gate into the back garden, where on the grass a party of staring dolls, tilting teddies and soft toys were being served miniature teacups by Lizzie.

"How many sugars would you like?" said Lizzie to a penguin wearing a bobble-hat.

"Hello, lovie," waved Eva from her sun-lounger.

The tubs of flowers that Mum had set on the concrete seemed to fade next to Eva. Her face was barely visible beneath huge, red-framed sunglasses and a large-brimmed, yellow hat. Pendulous silver earrings jangled as she stood up and David could see she was wearing a tent-like, multi-coloured sundress that showed a lot of chest and back. He was pleased to see her but relieved she hadn't met him from school.

"Where's Mum?"

"Ah," said Eva, "she's been called away."

"I thought she wasn't on call again till next week," said David. "She only finished night-shift yesterday."

"Oh no," said Eva. "Not by the hospital. She's had to go down to your grandad in Dorset. Come on, let's have a cup of tea and I'll tell you all about it."

"Just got to check something first," said David, throwing his bag onto the kitchen floor. "Be back in a minute," and he ran into the garden and disappeared into the garage.

"None in the freezer," he said as he returned and helped himself to four custard creams from the biscuit tin. "I'll have to ask Mum to get some."

"What are you talking about?" asked Eva. "Get some what?"

"Sausages. We need them for the camp-fire on Saturday."

Eva frowned. She disapproved of sausages, but instead of launching into her lecture on the evils of factory farming she said, "Your mum may not be back by then, David."

"She didn't say anything about going," said David with a mouthful of biscuit. "She only went at half-term. I bet she's all moody when she gets back."

Eva set two mugs of tea on the table. She'd removed her sunglasses and hat now but was having trouble with stray tendrils of wiry hair that were escaping from their combs.

"Do you remember your Nan Robinson, David?"

"Only a bit, from when I was little. Can you lend me some money then, till Mum gets back?"

"Money? What for?"

"Sausages. I told you. We need them for Saturday. Unless Mark's mum's got some. I'll find out tonight."

"Listen, David," said Eva. "Your nan's been taken ill – this morning. She's had a stroke and she's been rushed into hospital. That's why your mum had to dash off in such a hurry."

"When's she coming back then?" he asked, spooning out a biscuit that he'd over-dunked.

"We'll know more this evening, when she phones."

"Does Dad know then?"

"She rang him at school before she left. He'll be home as soon as he can, but he's got a parents' meeting at four. But don't worry – I've promised to stay over. Eva will look after you all, even if it means forking out for your disgusting sausages. But don't expect me to cook them; in fact, don't even let me get a whiff of them because . . ."

But David was already half-way up the stairs, ripping off his school uniform and wondering where he'd left his sweatshirt.

"You haven't seen my trainers anywhere, have you, Eva?" he called on his way downstairs. He ran into the kitchen, pausing just long enough to stuff a packet of crisps and a Mars bar into his pocket, and ran out through the back door.

"Hey, hold on a minute, I'm getting supper soon," shouted Eva.

"Save it for me," called David. "Important meeting. Be back about seven."

And before she had time to answer, he had disappeared into the garage, emerging seconds later, pedalling his bike down the path in his wellingtons.

"It says here that a skilled survival expert could live off the land indefinitely. That if society collapsed, only the self-sufficient would survive," mumbled David between the bites of Mars bar as he studied the pages of *Survival For Beginners*.

Mark heaved the wheelbarrow of sticks and cones backwards over the knotted tree roots, staggered to the wood pile, and stopped to get his breath back.

"You're supposed to be helping with this," he gasped, after a while.

"Good leaders know when to delegate," said David without looking up. "Here, listen to this. 'Young squirrels can be roasted or stewed and have a good flavour.'" He turned the page. "'All British snails are edible,'" he continued. "'All you have to do is feed them on lettuce for a few days to clear out their intestines.' And there's a recipe here for nettle soup. That's it!" he declared. "Nettle soup, roast squirrel and snail jelly. Yum, yum."

By now, Mark was writhing on the ground, holding

his stomach.

"I think I'm going to be sick," he grimaced.

"Wait a minute," said David. "It says here that roast swan has a tender, dark flesh and tastes of fish."

"I hate fish," said Mark.

"Pity," said David. 'We could have nipped down to the Library Gardens and bagged a couple. No, on second thoughts, not a good idea. It says that they're the property of the Queen and protected by . . ."

David was stopped in mid-sentence as a fir-cone hit him neatly on the ear. He looked up to see Mark, with an armful of cones, poised for attack.

"Hey, that's not fair. You've got all the ammunition," yelled David, leaping to his feet.

"Here's some more then," shouted Mark and aimed another cone.

"War!" yelled David and ten minutes later half the contents of the wheelbarrow lay scattered across the grass.

"Hi, Dad," said David, walking into the kitchen.

Dad was sitting at the table, going through a pile of record cards.

"Good grief," he said, looking up. "It's Stig of the Dump."

Eva took David's supper from the oven and set a place for him, then returned to her end of the table. Coils of silver, glass beads, stones, rings, clasps and studs peeped and glinted from boxes and trays before her. It was from these she made the bangles, earrings, brooches and necklaces that she sold from various market stalls.

Lizzie, dressed in her pyjamas and clasping her penguin, watched rapturously.

"These are my very favourites," said Lizzie, picking up a pair of earrings with pink and blue butterflies. "Could you make me some, Eva? Plee-ase?"

Eva picked them up, uncoiled the silver wire from the studs with her little tweezers, replaced them with clips, deftly secured them in place with a twist of her tiny pliers, leaned forward, and gently snapped them onto Lizzie's ears.

"There you are, lovie. But for dressing up only. Not for school."

Lizzie shrieked with delight and ran to examine them in the hall mirror.

"There's onion in this flan," said David, pushing three minuscule slivers to the side of his plate.

"Onions are good for you," said Eva. "Carbohydrate. Gives you energy."

"I hate onions."

"How do you know if you've never tasted them?"

"I just know," he said as he dissected the remainder of the flan with the concentration of a bomb-disposal expert defusing a bomb.

"I love onions, don't I, Eva?" said Lizzie.

"You would," said David. "I expect even your penguin loves onions."

"Don't be silly," said Lizzie. "Everyone knows penguins don't eat onions."

"I don't believe it," said Dad, studying a folder. "Just listen to some of these names in my tutor group next year – Androcles Jarvis and Zorah Buckle. Where do parents get these names from?"

"I like unusual names," said Eva. "They give character."

"Yes, I noticed that," said Dad rubbing his nose. "Growing up in Penge with the name of Phileas was extremely character-building."

Dad liked to show off his flattened nose occasionally and tell the story of how he'd defended his name against the legendary Norman Stebbings. Norm's dimensions and toughness seemed to increase on each telling, till in David's imagination, he'd taken on the image of King Kong.

"It was that film," confided Eva to David. "*Around the World in Eighty Days* – it came out the year your dad was born. I thought how wonderful it would be to have a son like Phileas Fogg, an adventurer and a traveller. I could just see us floating off together in our balloon. The trouble is you see, Phil's a typical Virgo. I hadn't planned on a Virgo. Very conscientious and studious are Virgos, but not very adventurous."

The phone on the wall trilled.

"I'll get it," said Dad.

"Hello? Linda? How is she?"

There was a long pause as Dad listened, head down.

"Yes, I know," he nodded. "But it had to happen some time. How's he taken it? And what about you? How are you?"

Eva, David and Lizzie watched in silence.

"Look, hold on, Linda," Dad interrupted. "Lizzie wants to say goodnight – she's waited up especially. I'll put her on, O.K.?"

Dad held out the phone and Lizzie ran forward, her butterfly earrings swinging.

"Mummy, Eva made me some earrings – with butterflies. She made them for my very own."

"Yes. I am. VERY good."

"I even helped with the washing-up."

"Yes, I promise."

"Mummy, when are you coming home?"

"All right then."

"Night, night."

She made two kissing noises and gave the phone back to Dad.

"Up to bed now, Lizzie," he said. "I'll be up in a minute."

"Come along, lovie," said Eva, taking her hand. "Let's find a safe place to put your earrings.'

"No, we're all fine," continued Dad on the phone.

There was another long pause, as he listened and nodded and made the occasional "mmm".

"So, when's it arranged for? Monday?"

"What about Lizzie?"

"No, you're right. I'll ask Eva to have her."

"Is there anything we can do this end?"

"Well, let us know the arrangements. And try not to worry."

"O.K., love. Look after yourself. I'll give you a ring tomorrow."

He replaced the receiver on the wall.

"Oi, I wanted a word with Mum," said David. "About the sausages. You could have asked me."

But Dad was standing deep in thought, hands in pockets.

"No need to go up straightaway," said Eva as she returned. "She's fast asleep already. What's the news from Linda?"

"Estelle died this afternoon," said Dad. "The funeral's on Monday, so she's staying on."

"Perhaps now he can have some sort of normal life," sighed Eva.

"Who?" asked David.

"I'll make some coffee," said Eva.

"Come and sit down," said Dad to David. "Eva told you your Nan Robinson had been taken ill and gone into hospital?"

He nodded.

"Well, she died this afternoon. She's been ill for a long time but it's still a bit of a shock. Your grandad's had to look after her for years."

"So, when's Mum coming home?"

"Well, the funeral's arranged for Monday. She's decided to stay on till then. There's a lot to be sorted out."

"Can't Grandad do that then?"

Eva set a tray of mugs in front of them.

"I expect he's a bit upset at the moment," she said. "You can't think straight at a time like this. He'll need your mum for a few days. They were married a long time you know, over forty years."

David was aware of them both studying him. He knew he ought to say something, like how sorry he was, but he couldn't. He didn't feel anything. His first thought had been how dreadful it must have been to be married to someone like Nan Robinson for forty years. If it meant Mum didn't have to go dashing off to Wimborne every couple of months, it was quite a relief.

"Was she very old then?" he asked at last.

"No, not very old. About sixty-five, I think," said Dad.

He turned to Eva. "Linda asked if you could look after Lizzie on Monday. She's too young for the funeral – it's best she stays at home."

"Does that mean I've got to go?" moaned David.

"Of course," said Dad and David could hear irritation in his voice. "And it's about time you started to think of other people instead of just yourself."

Chapter Two

"Eva, are you sure you haven't seen my trainers anywhere?" called David as he delved into the cupboard under the stairs on Monday morning.

"Save your efforts," called Dad from the kitchen. "You're not wearing trainers to the funeral. And you're not wearing those either," he said, pointing to David's jeans and tee-shirt.

"But I haven't got anything else."

"Then put on your school trousers, shirt and shoes. Don't forget to give them a polish first. And I want to see a tie too."

"Aw, Dad."

"Now."

"We'll see you tonight then, Phil," said Eva as she helped Lizzie with her cardigan and picked up the lunch-box from the worktop.

"I expect you'll be gone by the time I get back. Tell Linda not to worry about any shopping. I'll stock up for her and I'll have a meal ready for you when you get back. Give Daddy a kiss, lovie," she said to Lizzie.

"Give my love to Linda," she called from the back door, and then they were gone.

They hadn't even reached the M25 when the batteries

in David's Walkman failed. He'd brought a book but wasn't in the mood for it. They were waiting at yet another set of traffic lights, filtering one-way traffic past roadworks. The car grew hotter and hotter each time they stopped. He tried opening the window, but the traffic fumes were as bad as the heat.

He wondered about the funeral; he'd never been to one before. He remembered a film he'd seen on television where the open coffin had been displayed on the kitchen table and the family had gathered round to pay their last respects. He hoped he wouldn't have to look at his Nan Robinson.

Dad put the radio on. It was a programme about taxes and things called stocks and bonds and Tessas. It was Dad's favourite programme: he always tuned into it on Saturday mornings too, so David knew his chances of getting him to re-tune to Radio One were zero.

He found half a Polo mint in his trouser pocket and ate it. It was mushy and tasted of fabric softener.

He started to design the shelter: they'd use the old fence panels that Mark's dad had given them, though they'd need to line it with polythene to make it waterproof. They should have been doing it today, after school. Why did they make him come? He'd never liked Nan, anyway.

They had left the motorway now. Gradually, the dense lines of traffic gave way to open roads, sloping fields and trees. They passed a sign saying 'Ringwood'.

"Not far to Wimborne now," said Dad.

Twenty minutes later they were pulling up outside a small, neat brick house.

"Remember this?" asked Dad. "You weren't quite five when you last came here. I expect you've forgotten it all."

David peered out of the car window. There was something familiar about it. Dim images were forming in his head, like those pictures in Lizzie's magic drawing pad. There was an image of a camel, and something else too. Swans – swans floating on water.

The curtain in a window moved and Mum's face appeared. She waved and a minute later the side gate opened and there she was. Except she didn't quite look like Mum. She had tied her hair back from her face and was wearing a dark dress he hadn't seen before. She looked like someone else's mum, not his.

She bent down to kiss him as he climbed out of the car.

"My, you do look smart," she said.

"So do you."

"Come on, then – Grandad's inside. I've got some lunch ready." Then to Dad, "The cars are arriving at two."

He was relieved to see as he stepped through the back door that there was no coffin on the kitchen table. Grandad was sitting in an armchair in the corner, a newspaper spread across his lap, on which he was polishing his shoes. He looked up at David and stared hard.

"I'll make some tea," said Mum.

"So this is David," said Grandad at last.

"He's grown a lot since you last saw him," said Mum as she filled the kettle.

"Makes no difference," said Grandad. "I'd have picked him out in a crowd, anywhere."

"Give Grandad a kiss then," said Mum.

David felt awkward as he moved over to Grandad's chair and bent down to kiss his cheek. The smell of his skin sent David searching in his memory for the connection. It was shaving soap: the one that on Mum's suggestion he sent to Grandad every Christmas. Royal something – no, not royal. Imperial – Imperial Leather Shaving Stick.

Mum set the teapot on the table and they sat down to eat. He looked around the room and was surprised by how much he remembered. He saw the old stone sink and the checked curtain on a wire beneath it and it seemed that he could smell potato peelings, cabbage stalks and tealeaves. He'd hidden there once and there'd been a large, metal bucket under the sink full of them. There was the wallpaper with its design of forks and spoons and knives and the clock that looked like a plate. Behind the pots of geraniums on the window ledge, was a pair of stripy curtains that had once hung in the bathroom at home.

Grandad hardly spoke, and Mum and Dad were taking it in turns to fill the silence.

"Are you sure you don't want any more, Dad? There's plenty left," Mum was asking, and Dad filled them in with details of the journey, the roadworks and the appalling driving of a man in a white van.

David could feel Grandad looking at him and he couldn't stop himself nervously flicking back the heavy fringe of hair that kept flopping forward over his eyes, even though he'd combed it back with a wet comb and a blob of Mum's hair mousse.

He looked at the plate clock. I've only been here twenty-five minutes, he thought. It seemed like hours.

He helped clear away the table and offered to help with the wiping up: anything to pass the time. Dad went off to check the oil level in the car and Grandad went to change.

He wandered out to the garden. Beyond a paved area, five steps led to a tidy lawn where the scent of roses drifted from the borders. A leafy, flower-covered trellis stretched from a greenhouse across the lawn to an archway. He followed the path through the arch and there, on the other side, lay a vegetable and fruit garden set out in immaculate, neat rows. David could recognise the lettuce easily, and the onions resting on the soil, the leaves bent over at right angles and the pinkish, pearly globes drying in the sun. Not all of the leaves and shapes were so familiar. Mum bought all of her vegetables wrapped in polythene from the supermarket. But even he could recognise blackcurrant and gooseberry and raspberry bushes when he saw them. He picked a handful of fat raspberries and enjoyed their warm, juicy taste.

"David, are you there?" Mum called from the back door. "Come and give me a hand."

As he returned through the archway, David could see Grandad standing at the top of the steps, looking down at him. He was a tall man, but thinner than David remembered, his hair whiter too. His trousers hung loosely at the waist where his braces pulled them high and the stiff collar of his shirt stood away from his thin neck. He turned away before David reached him and went into the house.

Mum was setting out the table with plates and cutlery.

"Ah, there you are. Help put these out will you, David?"

She nodded to the worktop where plastic-sealed plates of sandwiches, rolls, pastries, cold meats and salads were standing.

"What's all this for?" asked David.

"Well, after the funeral everyone will come back here for a bite to eat and a cup of tea."

"Who's everyone?"

"Well, all the people going to the service. It's usual, you know, to meet afterwards and offer people food and drink."

"What, like a party?"

"No, not like a party exactly."

"How long will it take then?"

Mum gave David an impatient look. "A couple of hours or so."

Another couple of hours. Why had they made him come anyway? Grandad had barely said a word, Mum was busy with preparations and Dad had done his usual disappearing trick to the car.

"We'll be ready to leave in about twenty minutes," said Mum as she tucked some napkins into a vase. "When you've put everything onto the table, you'd better go and have a wash. Bathroom's upstairs, first door on the left."

"Is SHE upstairs?"

"Who?" said Mum, looking puzzled.

"You know, Nan Robinson."

"Oh, I see," said Mum. "No, of course not. The coffin's at the undertakers. They'll bring it here, in the hearse. We'll follow by car."

As David reached the door, she called him back.

"Come here, David."

She took both of his hands and looked at him.

"Look, I know this is all pretty boring for you, but just bear with it, will you? He may not show it, but your Grandad's very fond of you. He's missed seeing you all these years you know. Go on, then," she said, pushing back the hair from his face, "hurry up."

As David ran back down the stairs from the bathroom, he saw the camel. A camel sitting in the desert, behind which crouched a mother and her child, while an Arab in flowing robes stood before them, rifle ready to defend them from approaching riders who were brandishing spears and guns. It was a picture painted onto the glass door of a rectangular, wooden clock, hanging on the wall at the foot of the stairs. The same camel he'd remembered in the car. He remembered now being held up by Grandad so that he could turn the little knob on the door, open it and see inside as the round, brass pendulum swung from side to side.

"Go on," said Grandad from behind him. "You remember how to open it."

David opened the door. There was the swinging pendulum, the two heavy weights hanging either side, and the winding key, hanging on its little hook. It whirred, vibrated and a little hammer struck the gong twice.

"Ten minutes yet, Phil," said Grandad as Dad came hurrying in with oily hands. "Always like to keep it running ten minutes fast."

Chapter Three

"Coo-ee," called a voice from the back door. "I've brought the trifle I promised. And there are some cheese scones, too."

"Oh, come in, Auntie Bird," called Mum. "You know you don't have to stand on ceremony."

"How are you, dear?" said Auntie Bird, putting down her dishes. "Now, is there anything else I can do, Linda? You only have to ask – and this can't be David!" she exclaimed, throwing her arms around him and clasping him to her ample chest. "My goodness, you've grown since I saw you last year."

When David was finally released from her embrace and could come up for air, he realised that he was now able to look down at Auntie Bird. He hadn't been able to do that when she'd called on them last summer. She always came to see them when she visited her sister who lived nearby in Beckenham.

"No thanks. I think we're almost ready," said Mum, checking her hair in a little mirror above the sink, and picking up her shoulder bag.

"The cars are here," called Dad from the front door. And as David followed them onto the pavement, he thought Auntie Bird looked just like a sparrow, her short plump body on two impossibly thin ankles, bobbing along the path.

Dad and David drove behind the long black car ahead of them. David could see the back of Mum's head, Grandad's white hair, and Auntie Bird's hat through the rear window.

The hearse containing the wreath-covered coffin and its solemn-looking driver and attendants led the slow procession.

"Auntie Bird's a strange sort of name," said David.

"Your mum has always called her that," said Dad. "From when she was a child. Mrs Bird has lived next door to your grandparents for years. She's not a relative, of course, but she's become like part of the family, especially after – well, after your Nan became ill. You didn't call adults by their Christian names when we were children, you know. High treason that would have been."

David did not know any of the dozen or so mourners who stood at the graveside. He stared at the coffin that lay across several planks above the freshly dug grave.

The vicar's voice droned on. "Some of you remember Estelle's laughter and joy of life and we pray that her soul will again find that joy, and peace too, for life . . ."

Laughter and joy? Was this Nan Robinson he was talking about?

Keeping his head down, he looked sideways up at

Mum. Her head was bowed and her face was screwed up, trying to hold something back. Then he saw the tears start to trickle down her face, and she was struggling with her bag, trying to find a tissue. Dad produced a handkerchief from his pocket, gave it to her, and put his arm around her. Mrs Bird too was dabbing her eyes. But Grandad just stood, head bowed, as immobile as a statue.

David was embarrassed that he could not feel any emotion. It would have been different if it was Eva, or Mum or Dad or Lizzie. Not so long ago there had been an item on the television news about a motorway pile-up and a girl of about his age had been the only survivor from her family. He'd lain awake at night, worrying that it might happen to him. It had made his throat ache just thinking about it. But not now, not for Nan Robinson, who was truly dead, lying there in her coffin.

The vicar had stopped talking now and the coffin was being lowered into the ground by long straps. Then people started to move slowly away, going up to Grandad and Mum or standing to talk.

He turned away, reading the dates on the gravestones. He liked to work out how long people had lived, who'd outlived who and by how many years.

IN LOVING MEMORY OF
HENRY ARTHUR LEWINSON
BORN 25th April 1897 – DIED
1st November 1965

Sixty-eight years old, thought David.

ALSO BEATRICE MARY LEWINSON
BELOVED WIFE, MOTHER AND
GRANDMOTHER
BORN 1st February 1902 – DIED
30th September 1976

Aged seventy-four. Outlived Henry by almost exactly eleven years.

Gradually, the mourners started to move slowly along the path back to the cars. David followed.

He was bored and feeling full-up. But there wasn't much else to do except eat. They were in the front room where people sat on the old settee and armchairs or the wooden chairs brought from the kitchen. There was a damp, unused smell. Most of the visitors were old, like the room, with its cold, bulky furniture and its lacy cloths on the chair arms and backs. Auntie Bird and Mum were bustling in and out with trays of tea and Dad was talking to the vicar. To relieve the monotony, David had helped pass round the plates of sandwiches and rolls, but he'd tired of being asked what his favourite subject was at school, or what he wanted to be when he grew up, though Mum had given him a grateful smile and he'd heard one old lady tell her what a helpful, polite boy he was.

"Like two peas in a pod," he heard a woman say to an old man, "that David's the image of . . ."

As he tried to squeeze past them she hesitated for a moment and moved aside. "Lovely trifle," she commented as she smiled to let him through.

Who was he the image of, he wondered as he helped himself to a scone from the kitchen. Certainly not Dad. David was growing so fast he would soon be looking down on Dad's bald patch. He hadn't quite got used to this growth spurt. It was as if his brain had lost control of his feet. He was always tripping over himself and the scars on his knees bore the evidence.

He strolled out into the garden. The door of the greenhouse was open and he wandered in. Trays of fresh green seedlings ranged along the staging down one side, and on the other side tomatoes in various shades between green and red, and cucumbers from finger-size to ready-to-eat-size, hung in abundance. The pungent, warm, peppery smell hung heavily in the air. He continued on, following the path through the fruit and vegetable garden, past the shed to a thick row of runner beans at the bottom.

There was a gap between the bean row and the fence and he went through. Then he stopped and stared, for there was the other image he'd recalled in the car. A swan, a swan floating on water, then another, followed by four half-grown cygnets, still showing the remains of their grubby brown plumage. For just beyond the grassy area where he was now standing, on the other side of a gated fence, was the river. It was as if he was re-watching an old film. You thought you'd forgotten it, but slowly each image released the memory of another. He knew that the shed he'd just passed had an upside-down keyhole: he remembered being shown how to unlock it with a large, black key.

He knew that behind the shed was the compost heap where he had helped Grandad empty the bucket from under the sink.

He walked back to the shed and peered in, but the sunlight was reflecting on the windows, and apart from some ropes of onions hanging against the glass, all he could make out was the dim outline of crammed shelves.

"Your mother's looking for you."

David turned to see Grandad, now in shirt-sleeves and braced trousers, standing on the path. He moved to one side to let him pass, but David knew that he'd been watching him all the time.

"I won't hear of it," Auntie Bird was saying as she squeezed washing-up liquid into the sink. "You've done quite enough and you've a long journey ahead of you. Peggy and Marjorie will give me a hand. It'll all be done in a jiffy."

Two white-haired women, (Peggy and Marjorie, David guessed), were scraping plates and re-applying plastic film to plates of left-overs.

"I can't just go and leave it all to you," Mum protested, gathering up the tablecloth and shaking it out of the door.

"Nonsense," insisted Auntie Bird, taking the cloth from her. "Look, here's David, all ready to go, and Phil's got work tomorrow. The earlier the start you make, the better."

Mum did look tired, David thought and her eyes were red and puffy.

"She's right," said Grandad, who had appeared in the doorway, holding Mum's case and her coat. "You get yourself back home."

Defeated, Mum picked up her handbag.

"Are you absolutely sure? I hate leaving all this mess."

Dad picked up the case and led the way out to the car.

"You'll look after yourself, won't you, Dad?" said Mum, stretching up to kiss his cheek. "You'll ring if you need anything? Look, are you sure you won't come back with us? The spare room's always there for you, any time you want."

"I'll keep my beady eye on him, don't you worry," said Auntie Bird as she gave everyone her customary squeeze.

"David, say goodbye to Grandad," said Mum.

"Goodbye, lad," said Grandad but before David had time to respond with his embarrassed kiss, Grandad had turned back to the house.

They drove along in silence. David could see Mum's reflection in the nearside mirror, staring out of the window, but as if she wasn't seeing anything beyond the glass.

"Auntie Bird doesn't change, does she?" said Dad eventually. "At least she's there to keep an eye on him. Thank God for the Auntie Birds of this world."

"I'd forgotten about the river," said David. "You were dead lucky having a river at the bottom of your garden, Mum. I wish we had one. You could build rafts and things."

"Mmmm," said Mum as if she wasn't really listening.

David sat in the back of the car, thinking about all the things he would do if he had a river in the bottom of his garden.

"This will be the first night Dad's been on his own," said Mum suddenly. "I can't help worrying."

"He's looked after himself and your mother for years," said Dad. "He's perfectly capable of looking after himself."

"That's what bothers me," said Mum. "You don't know what it's been like these last few days – Auntie Bird and I did everything. He just withdrew. He's never been like that, he's always been so independent, so in charge of things. It was dreadful to see him so passive."

"What exactly was wrong with Nan Robinson?" asked David.

"She had a stroke," said Mum.

"No, before that?"

"She was ill."

"I know, but what with?"

"Oh, for heaven's sake," cried Mum, pressing her fingers against her forehead, "I've got a splitting headache and all you can do is ask questions!"

"There's a café about a mile ahead," interrupted

Dad. “Let’s stop and have some coffee and you can take a couple of aspirin.”

He switched on the radio just in time to catch the bleeps announcing the six o’clock news.

It seemed to David that days had passed since they’d set off from home to the funeral.

Chapter Four

David had to run to school on Tuesday morning. It was all Mum's fault. She'd gone through his school bag and found a rotten apple and several letters from school that he'd forgotten to pass on. He would have remembered eventually, but she'd had to go on about it and had made him late.

It wasn't even as if they were about anything important: just a reminder about the end of term concert, a list of dates for next term and details of the school uniform he'd be needing at his new school in September.

Then, when he got home after school, Mum was waiting for him in the kitchen. He could tell she was cross about something. He looked around for a clue.

"Recognise these?" she said removing something from a plastic bag by the pedal bin.

"My trainers?" said David.

"You tell me," she demanded angrily. "I believe they were trainers once. The problem is that after being left out in the garden for nearly a week in all weathers, they're now just a soggy mess of rubber and leather."

She threw them into the bin. David waited. He knew from experience she was just warming up and it was best if he remained quiet with a suitably apologetic expression.

"Thirty-five pounds they cost!" she exploded. "Do you think money grows on trees? Did it not occur to you to look for them?"

She started to throw her arms about.

"I just don't understand it. How come you can recite the complete biography of every astronaut who's lived, yet can't remember where you've left your trainers? Which brings me to something else – my new frying-pan, and my tin-opener. I can't find them anywhere. Eva suggested you might know something about them. Well?"

She stood, hands on hips, glaring at him.

"Ah," said David, remembering. "I'm sorry, Mum. I borrowed them for the camp. They must be at Mark's."

"I don't believe it," she said. "That's the last straw. Just you get over there and fetch them this minute."

"But he's gone to the dentist," said David.

"I don't care if he's gone to the moon, you just get over there and don't you dare come back without them!"

He turned to go.

"And your new trainers can come out of your savings," she called. "Perhaps that will improve your memory."

It was worse when he got back and she saw the frying-pan. The outside that had once been shiny steel, was now black, and the inside which had once been black, had lots of shiny marks where his fork had scraped the sausages off. Bits of soggy sausage and egg white were still clinging to the pan.

"I couldn't find the tin-opener," said David.

She threw the pan into the washing-up bowl.

"Just get out of my sight!" she shouted.

During the last week of school, the timetable collapsed beneath rehearsals for the end-of-term concert, finishing off projects, tidying and clearing up, and preparations for the end-of-term disco.

Mark and David expressed the opinion that the last week of term was a waste of time and it would be more sensible to let them all stay home and have an extra week of holiday. But Warren pointed out that it wouldn't solve the problem.

"Look, if you do that, then the previous week, which would now be the LAST week, would be taken up in just the same way. You could go on for ever, adding weeks on to the holidays, till the year was one long holiday. Then, where would you be?"

"Warren," chorused David and Mark in unison. "Shut up."

Emotions were running high. Packs of wet-eyed girls clasping tissues and autograph books roamed the corridors and classrooms, hunting members of staff, even complete strangers, to sign the pastel pages of their books.

Mr Hilton, the headmaster, was forced to give a stern lecture at assembly about bad sportsmanship, following the staff-versus-children netball match, when a group from 6H had booed after Mr Jones had scored his fifth goal.

Shaun Brodie was on report for writing something rude in the boys' toilets. To everyone's disappointment, it had been scrubbed off by the caretaker before they'd had a chance to read it and there was much speculation as to what he'd written. Shaun just grinned smugly when asked, cracked his nose and said, "Give us 50p first," so it remained a mystery. Mark requested that he used indelible ink next time. "I might, I might not," he answered after they'd explained what indelible meant.

By the end of the week, Mum's mood had still not improved. She was not so much bad-tempered though, as pre-occupied, and she looked worn out. She'd lost her car keys and had to cancel her dentist's appointment. Lizzie came home with them: she'd found them in her lunch-box, beneath her peanut-butter sandwiches.

Part of the reason, David knew, was because of Auntie Bird's phone call on Wednesday.

"It's just what I thought," said Mum to Dad. "He's not looking after himself. Even Auntie Bird's concerned. She hasn't seen him in the garden for days. I shall have to go down again."

"I don't think that's the answer," said Dad patiently.

"You won't be able to do any more than Auntie Bird and you're going to wear yourself out with all this to-ing and fro-ing."

"Well, you just tell me what the answer is!" Mum had shouted as she drained the spaghetti down the sink. The lid slipped, and the whole lot cascaded into the washing-up bowl, draping the dirty coffee cups in their soapy water. They had to make do with beans on toast that evening.

David had been looking forward to Friday, the last day of term. It had been the deadline they'd given themselves to finish preparations for the camp. But instead of the customary last-day thrill of excitement that usually announced the beginning of the holidays, David felt empty and flat. Earlier in the week, he and Mark had teased the tearful girls and their autograph books, but now that the last day had finally arrived, he realised that he was leaving behind a large part of his life: the security of a place and faces he'd known since his first day of school. They were all moving on to different schools, going their separate ways to unknown worlds.

As he cycled to Mark's that evening, he had a strange feeling of detachment, as if he didn't really belong anywhere.

But half-an-hour later, as they lay inside the shelter, peering up at the sunlight filtering through the slats, things looked different.

"Bring your sleeping bag in the morning," said

Mark. "We'll sleep here tomorrow night."

"Five whole weeks," said David, punching the air. "Five weeks of sleeping under the stars!"

The mood improved when after supper, in the sitting room, Dad produced several boxes of chocolates: end-of-term presents from school leavers. It always signalled the start of the holidays.

David was munching a hazelnut twirl when the phone rang.

When Mum returned a few minutes later, there was no need to ask who it was from or what it was about.

"It can't be that bad," said Dad, trying to cheer her up and offering her favourite caramel cup.

She waved it away.

"He's let it all go," she said, flopping down into the armchair and pushing her fingers through her hair. "Everything. The greenhouse hasn't been opened all week or watered. Everything is dead or dying. The same with the fruit – left to rot on the bushes. He hasn't touched a thing since we left. Auntie Bird said the left-overs are still in the fridge, going mouldy. He won't even let her help, says he's perfectly all right."

She stared at the ceiling.

"Look, perhaps we could try again to persuade him to come here for a week or two . . ."

"Auntie Bird's tried – it's no good. He's as stubborn as a mule. You know, she's even cancelled her visit to her sister in Beckenham, she's that worried."

"I imagine he feels it's all a waste of time," said Dad. "He's got no one to do it for, now that Estelle's gone.

Not that he ever got any thanks from her. But I suppose she gave him a purpose."

Dad sealed the box of chocolates and put it on the mantelpiece.

They sat there saying nothing. Nan Robinson seemed to have the same dampening effect in death as in life.

"There's got to be something we can do," said Mum.

David was coming out of the bathroom, his hair wet from the shower, when he heard Mum's voice. Her bedroom door was slightly open and she was talking to someone on the phone.

"I hate having to ask, Dad, but I'm at my wit's end. I know you've got other things on your mind, but I don't know who else to ask."

"No – Eva's off to Wales on Sunday . . ."

"It would be such an enormous help."

David started to walk away, then stopped in his tracks.

"No – just David. Now that the holidays are here, he doesn't know what to do with himself. If you could have him, just for a week, say . . ."

What was she talking about?

"It's just that we can't afford a proper holiday this year, what with the roof needing doing, and he gets so bored . . ."

"Yes, I know that, but you needn't go to any extra trouble . . ."

"Well, we could put him on the coach at Victoria – if you could meet him at Poole, say on Monday . . ."

"No, he'd like to get to know you better, you said yourself you hardly know him."

"You will? Oh, Dad, thanks! Now, are you sure? Oh, you don't know how much this means."

"Well, we'll sort that out later. Look, I'll give you a call tomorrow, when I've found out the coach times. Dad, you're wonderful!"

He heard the phone click. Mum almost ran out of the room. It was the first time he'd seen her smile in over a week. But when she saw David, she stopped.

"I heard!" he shouted. "I heard it all. And I'm not going. You can't make me!"

He ran into his room and threw himself across his bed. It was the first time he'd cried since he was nine when he'd broken his arm.

Chapter Five

The London to Poole coach pulled out of Victoria Station. Mum, Dad and Lizzie waved and David managed to return a tight smile.

Fifteen minutes later, the coach had travelled less than a mile and was queuing behind a tangle of traffic.

"Don't worry if you're late," Mum had said. "Grandad will be waiting to meet you. Give us a ring to let us know you've arrived safely."

It was Dad though, who had knocked on his door on Friday night, after the phone call.

"Go away!" David had yelled.

But Dad had come in anyway.

"Leave me alone!" he'd shouted, burying his head under the pillow.

Dad sat on the bed and waited.

"You can't make me go!" cried David's muffled voice through the pillow.

"No," said Dad at last. "You're perfectly right. We can't make you go. What's more, we wouldn't want to try."

David rolled over. He wiped his nose on his sleeve. Dad pulled a hankie from his pocket and handed it over.

"It's not fair. I hate her. I know perfectly well what to do in the holidays. Why is she lying? She knows all about the camp. It's just not fair!"

"No," said Dad. "You're right again. It's not fair. That's one of the signs of growing up – the discovery that things aren't fair."

"Then I don't have to go?"

"No, not if that's what you choose."

David sat up and hugged his knees.

"I still hate her."

"What?"

"Well, you don't expect your own mother to tell lies about you, behind your back."

"It's hard to understand, I know, but she did it for all the best reasons."

"Oh, yeh?" said David looking away. "Well, she still shouldn't tell lies, should she?"

"Not even when it's the only way of helping someone?"

"How can telling lies help anyone?"

"You remember earlier, when we were talking about Grandad? I said that he'd probably lost interest because he had no one to look after any more? Well, it made her think. Each time someone tries to help him, he turns them away. Perhaps we were doing it all wrong. Perhaps we should ask *him* for help – make him feel he was needed again."

"But I don't need help, or looking after!" shouted David, pounding the bed with his fists.

"We all know that," said Dad. "That's why she lied. And it worked. He's agreed. It could be the only way of really helping him."

"But she should have asked me first!"

"Absolutely. She should have asked you first. But she didn't. She acted on impulse."

"Then she shouldn't, should she?"

"I didn't notice you complaining at half-term, when on impulse, she dropped everything to take you and Mark to the Science Museum."

"That's different."

Dad looked at David, then said, "There's something else you should know, David. About your Nan Robinson. Her illness – well, it wasn't a physical illness she suffered from, but a mental one. Do you know what that means?"

"She was mad?"

"Not exactly – though she had to spend some long periods in hospital, but with drugs and your Grandad's care, it was possible for her to live at home. She certainly lost her grasp of reality, to the point when she sometimes behaved in an unpredictable way. That's why they stopped visiting here. But your Grandad never stopped caring for her, and now he's free to live a more normal life, he can't come to terms with it: he's not used to it. If helping him costs a small lie, then perhaps it's worth it."

He stood up. "Just think about it," said Dad. "We know how much this camp means to you. We understand if you don't want to give up a week of the holidays. No one's going to MAKE you do anything."

And no one did.

Later, when Mum came up to say goodnight, she

didn't mention it, just said she was sorry. He was right to be angry, it was an unforgivable thing to do.

The worst part had been telling Mark. He felt like a traitor.

As the coach drew into Poole Bus Station, he could see Grandad scanning the windows for him.

"So," said Grandad on the bus ride to Wimborne, "the problem is, you don't know what to do with yourself, is it?"

"Not exactly," said David, determined not to be thought of as a person who could not occupy himself, even if it was the excuse for his visit. "It's just that there were complications."

"This was your mum's room," said Grandad putting David's hold-all down.

David nodded and Grandad went downstairs.

It was a tiny room with a sloping ceiling, covered in a faded yellow, daisy-sprigged wallpaper. A high, wooden-ended bed stood against the wall opposite the window. It had a shiny pink quilt. David looked out the window but all he could see beyond the front garden's hedge were the roofs of the houses opposite.

He took his Walkman from his rucksack and stood it on the doily-covered table by his bed. The small armchair in the corner held a collection of dolls and soft toys. He picked up two small pigs: Pinky declared one of the pig's hats, Perky declared the other.

It was hard to imagine his mother as a child, playing

in this room. He knew a good deal about Dad's childhood from Eva, but he knew very little about Mum's.

He opened the cupboard in the alcove next to the fireplace. The inside of the door was covered with faded cut-outs and posters, the sellotape yellowed and curling. He'd heard of The Beatles and The Rolling Stones, but who were Herman's Hermits?

He took his time unpacking his few belongings. If he went downstairs too soon, he'd have to think of things to say and it was hard work. The journey on the bus had been mostly long silences. He put his drawing pad, pencils and books on the bed. He might need them this evening: he'd made contingency plans for a long and boring week.

He wandered into the bathroom next door and put his sponge bag on the window-sill. Grandad's shaving-brush and soap stood on a little ledge beneath a spotted mirror. The room smelt strongly of Imperial Leather. He stared at himself in the mirror: his 'mirror face' Mum called it, with one eyebrow raised quizzically and a lop-sided grin. He examined his teeth and peered up his nose. He pushed back his fringe. It flopped forward. He picked up the shaving-brush and pretended to lather his face with it. He lifted up his chin and stretched his neck, like he'd seen Dad do hundreds of times. Then he put on an evil, leering face, made a slicing movement with a finger across his neck, then grasping his neck, and muttering 'oh, no – it's Sweeney Todd the demon barber!' he staggered out into the passageway.

He stood there, hands in his shorts' pockets, wondering what to do next. There were two doors opposite. The one on the left was slightly ajar. He crossed the passage softly and gave it a gentle push. This must be Grandad's room: the same smell, the high, old-fashioned double bed and dark, old furniture. A pair of trousers with braces still attached hung from the back of a chair.

David pulled the door back to its original position and moved to the next door. He listened to make sure Grandad wasn't coming up the stairs and quietly turned the handle. The door was a little stiff, and creaked for the first couple of inches. The room was completely empty. Not a stick of furniture, no curtains, no carpet, just bare, worn lino and deep blue walls: his favourite colour. Yet in spite of its spartan appearance it seemed to welcome him. He stepped in. The ceiling sloped steeply on two sides. He touched them – they were warm. Must get the sun in here, thought David. But the best thing was the view. A long, low window with a deep ledge looked down onto the garden. He could see it all: the gated fence at the bottom, the river, and beyond the trees on the far side, the glimpse of a field.

He stretched himself out on the window seat. He'd much rather have this room. What a shame it didn't have any furniture. This is the best room in the house, thought David. Perhaps it had been Nan's. Mum said she'd been busy clearing out.

Suddenly, he caught sight of Grandad coming out of

the greenhouse. Feeling a little guilty about trespassing, David made to duck down but his movement must have made Grandad look up. David stared back. Grandad looked so surprised, that he took a step backwards, steadied himself, then looked again. It's no use pretending I'm not here, thought David and he gave a wave. Slowly, Grandad lifted his arm and waved back.

Grandad was washing tomatoes at the kitchen sink when David entered.

"Been exploring then, have you?" asked Grandad without turning round.

"Sorry," said David. "I should have asked."

"No need. Just made me jump a bit, that's all."

"Can I ring Mum?" asked David. "She said to let her know that I've arrived safely."

"After six o'clock. Cheap rate then."

He fetched a bowl from the dresser and put the tomatoes in it.

"Now," he said, "in this house we have dinner at dinner time – that's twelve o'clock, not in the evening like you're used to. Doesn't do my digestion any good, that. And we have tea at five o'clock. But because you've been on the coach, I'm making an exception, and we'll have dinner in about half an hour. Right? Good. That's sorted then. Now, make yourself useful. There's still some raspberries left. Go well with ice-cream, they will."

He handed David a metal colander.

"Off you go then."

"Wait," he called as David reached the door. "You do know what raspberries look like, I suppose?"

"Of course," said David. Then before he could stop himself, "... they grow in little plastic punnets, covered in polythene."

Grandad's mouth twitched with the smallest of smiles.

"That's enough of your cheek," he said.

"One more thing – no going near the river – saw a family of swans the other day and they can get quite nasty if you get too close. Keep to this side of the fence. Got it?"

"Got it," said David.

As David passed the greenhouse he could see what Mum had been talking about. There were only a few tomato and cucumber plants that had survived a week of neglect. The rest had vanished. As he trailed along the path he could see the soil between the neat vegetable rows was sprinkled with weeds, and the onions were still lying there. Darkened, rotting fruits hung from the bushes and scattered the ground. He filled the colander with raspberries and went to look for the swans but there was no sign of them. He noticed, though, the shrivelled remains of the seedlings and yellowing leaves of the cucumber and tomato plants, piled onto the compost. Grandad had certainly been busy these last couple of days.

"Nothing like home-grown raspberries," said Grandad.

"You're a good cook," said David.

"Years of practice. Now, you wash and I'll wipe and put away."

David carried the dirty plates to the sink, tipped them into the bowl and turned the tap.

"What's that supposed to be?" Grandad asked.

"You said, do the washing-up."

"Look," he said, removing everything from the bowl and tipping away the water. "There's a wrong and a right way of doing everything. Haven't you ever done the washing-up before?"

"We've got a dishwasher at home."

"Well, so have I now – you. Now watch. First we scrape off the plates, see?"

He pulled out the bucket from under the sink and scraped the plates with a knife.

"Anything for the compost goes in here. Next, we rinse everything under the tap."

He removed the bowl and demonstrated how to rinse a plate.

"Now we're ready for stage three," he said, replacing the bowl and filling it with hot, soapy water. David picked up the dish-cloth and reached for the saucepan.

"No, not that," said Grandad, taking it from him. "Glasses first, then plates, then cutlery, greasy things last. You'll soon get the hang."

Wowee, thought David. This is going to be some holiday. What was Mark doing now? I bet he's not doing stage three of the washing-up.

*

After David had rung Mum, Grandad appeared in his jacket and said, "Come along then. Time to get your bearings."

He led the way along the road, then right into an alleyway which led to a path that ran parallel to the river.

"This way into town," said Grandad, "along the River Allen."

Further on, as the path skirted the car park, a large sheet of polythene flapped gently from beneath the wheels of a supermarket trolley.

"Waste not, want not," said Grandad as he bent to retrieve it, folded it up neatly, and put it in his pocket. "Might come in useful."

The river widened as they reached a bridge, and as it did so, became shallower. It was so clear David could see the pebbles glinting on the bottom. Two boys were wading along, turning over the stones. A group of ducks watched leisurely from the other bank.

"See those towers," said Grandad, pointing across the road. "That's the Wimborne Minster. They say King Ethelred's buried there – King Alfred the Great's elder brother. Killed by the Danes was Ethelred."

They headed towards it and soon were standing on a large green, looking up at the grey and red bricks of the two church towers. David was more interested in a group of about his own age who were lolling on the grass and pushing each other off the stone wall. They looked as if they were enjoying themselves.

Grandad looked at his watch, pointed up to a window high up on the right-hand tower and said, "Keep your eye on that window – the left one."

David craned his neck and watched. Suddenly the window moved, the small figure of a soldier in white breeches, a red coat and a black cocked hat, wheeled into view. He raised both hands in turn and struck the bells on either side of him. DING DONG!

"The Quarter Jack," said Grandad. "Strikes every quarter-of-an-hour. Used to be a monk but they changed him to a grenadier during the war against Napoleon.

'How small the quarters of the hour march by
That Jack o'clock never forgets;
Ding dong;
Just so did he clang before I came
And so will clang when I'm gone,'"

recited Grandad.

David looked round furtively to make sure no one had heard.

"Know who wrote that?" he asked.

David didn't know many poets.

"Michael Rosen?" he guessed.

"Thomas Hardy. Used to live in Wimborne. Heard of him?"

David shook his head.

Grandad led the way through a narrow lane, coming out by Woolworths on the corner of a large open square surrounded by shops.

"You're walking on dead bodies here, David."

"What?"

"Dead bodies. Hundreds of them. Plague victims. This used to be a churchyard. They still dig up the bones from time to time, when they repair the road. And over there . . ." he pointed to an old house, ". . . that's where Gulliver lived. He was a famous smuggler."

They walked on. Dead kings, plague victims, rivers and bridges, famous smugglers and Danes. This place was beginning to sound quite interesting.

As they turned the corner into Byron Road, Auntie Bird was coming out of Grandad's front gate.

"Ah, so there you are!" she cried, hugging David. "Now, I've made a cake from a new W.I. recipe and I need someone to test it for me. How about it?"

They followed her bustling figure along the path and into her kitchen. It was very different to Grandad's with its white cupboards and red tiles. She led them to the sitting-room where big, sliding glass doors looked out onto her garden. David sank into a large velvety armchair as Auntie Bird set small tables before them.

"Now, David, what would you like to drink? There's tea, milk, coffee, home-made lemonade and I got in a bottle of cola too," she said counting them off on her fingers.

"It's a very good recipe," said David a little later, as he wiped the chocolate cream from his mouth.

"A third slice?" she offered.

But David was watching an enormously fat, tortoise-shell cat that had waddled into the room.

"Not for you, Blossom," said Auntie Bird, pushing its nose away from the cake.

"It's huge!" said David.

"Well, she's expecting, you see. She's adopted me – just walked in one day and decided to stay. I've put a notice in the Post Office window, but no one's claimed her. I think she'll have them any day now – she's made a nest in the cupboard under the stairs. I have to keep the vacuum cleaner in the hall now."

She cut another slice of cake.

"I shouldn't be eating this really. I'm trying to watch my weight. Now, has your grandad told you about Hannah?"

"Hannah?"

"Yes, my great-niece, lives off Allenview Road. I thought it would be nice for you to meet someone of your own age while you're here. Mmm?"

David groaned inwardly.

"Oh, yes. Thanks."

As they left, she said, "Rain forecast for tomorrow, George. You ought to try and get those onions in."

Grandad gave a mock salute. He'd hardly spoken a word all evening. That was one of the good things about Auntie Bird, thought David as he lay in bed. She'd done all the talking.

Chapter Six

David was surprised the next morning when he looked at his watch and saw that it was already ten past nine. He dressed and went downstairs.

"Sleep well?" asked Grandad who was sitting at the kitchen table, reading a newspaper.

"Yes thanks."

Grandad motioned him to sit down at the table where a spoon, bowl and mug were set out. He went over to the stove, turned on the gas and started to stir something in a saucepan. A few minutes later he brought it over to the table and poured it into David's bowl.

Porridge? In summer? What about cornflakes or muesli?

Grandad plunged the spoon into a tin of syrup and trailed it onto the porridge, then fetched a little jug from the fridge.

"Top of the milk," he said. "There you go."

"There's a bit more left in the pan," he said a few minutes later, looking over the top of his newspaper. "Help yourself." So he did.

David could see that Grandad had already been working on the garden. There was a wheelbarrow and hoe on the path and half the vegetable area had been cleared of weeds. Grandad handed him a wooden tray: "You can start picking up the onions. Auntie Bird's right – it'll rain soon." He looked up at the dark clouds gathering in the distance.

David had cleared the first row and had laid them along the slatted shelf in the greenhouse just as Grandad had shown him, where they could finish drying, when he saw Auntie Bird bobbing down the path towards them.

"I'm popping down to the Oxfam shop with a bundle of curtains," she said. "I thought, while I'm at it, I may as well take those boxes of Estelle's, the ones Linda and me sorted out."

Grandad straightened up. "No rush," he said.

Auntie Bird's lips tightened. David sensed that this had happened before and she was having another try.

"Nonsense," she insisted. "You don't want all those boxes gathering dust, especially when they could be put to good use. Come along, David," she said, heading towards the house. "You can help us carry them to my car."

David wasn't sure what to do. He looked to Grandad for the go-ahead.

"Interfering woman," he muttered, throwing down his hoe and following her.

"Shoes!" glared Grandad as David stepped into the kitchen in his soil-caked trainers.

He followed their voices, through the kitchen, into

the hall to the door opposite the sitting-room to the left of the front door. So this had been Nan's room: not the blue room upstairs.

"Oh, for goodness sake, let's have some light in here," Auntie Bird was saying as she tugged at the heavy brown velvet curtains that were partly drawn.

Even before he stepped in, the gloom and coldness reached him and then intensified. Just as the blue room had seemed to welcome him, this room seemed to set up a barrier. Eva believed in ghosts: she said she could sense atmospheres. Dad didn't, and they would have arguments about what Dad called "Putting unscientific ideas into children's heads". He knew that Dad was right, but there was something about this room that made him want to turn away. It's just the coldness of it, he told himself. The dark, heavy furniture, the grubby brown wallpaper, the empty bed with its piled up blankets and pillows.

"Turn the light on, David, I can't see for looking," said Auntie Bird. "This could be quite a nice room," she continued as she sorted through the bags and boxes. "Amazing what you can do with a lick of paint and new curtains. It's a pity Estelle never let you touch it. George, you take that big box. David, you bring that box of shoes."

But halfway across the room, the bottom of the box split open and the contents cascaded to the floor. He bent down and as he reached out for a slipper, he stopped. It was quite an ordinary slipper: brown plaid, with the edges buttoned back and grey bobbles. But it was all he could do to make himself pick it up. He flung it quickly into the box and as he did so, the words "He's a devil, an evil devil! Evil! Evil!" played in his head.

"What's the matter?" asked Auntie Bird, returning for another box.

"The box broke," said David.

"Well, I think I'm going to need some help with this," said Auntie Bird as she slammed the car boot. "I can't unload this lot on my own."

"We may as well come along," said Grandad. "I need to go in – I promised some onions to the green-grocers."

He went inside and returned a few minutes later in his jacket and cap and carrying a box of onions, just as large drops of rain began to spot the pavement.

"Blast it," said Grandad. "Hang on – the onions are still out, and my hoe."

"David can see to those, can't you, dear?" said Auntie Bird.

"I don't like leaving him on his own," said Grandad.

"I'll be O.K.," said David. He didn't fancy having to squeeze in the back seat with all those old clothes and shoes.

Grandad hesitated.

"Come along, George," said Auntie Bird, getting into the driver's seat. "We'll be back in less than half an hour."

David ran into the house and shut the front door.

For a moment he stood staring into Nan's room. Empty now of her clothes and possessions, yet he felt she hadn't really gone. He could almost see her, sitting in the cushioned armchair that squatted before the dead television set in the corner, its back to the window and the outside world. He leaned forward, grabbed the door handle and slammed it shut.

He'd done it just in time. Got all the onions in, put the hoe away, even emptied the wheelbarrow and stood it, end up as he'd seen it before, leaning against the side of the shed. His wet shirt was clinging to him and water was dripping off his fringe as he waited in the shed for the rain to ease off. It was sheeting down in torrents, pouring down the window and hammering on the roof.

It was a large shed but crammed from floor to ceiling with shelves, cupboards and tools. He started to explore, though it was now so dark that he had to peer closely. There was a long work-bench under the window, where tools hung from either side. At the door end spades, rakes, hoes and tools he couldn't name hung neatly, their well-polished steel dulled by the gloom. The other two sides were filled with floor cupboards and densely-packed shelves. Jars, tins, boxes and trays paraded their neatly labelled contents. NAILS – 2″, SCREWS – BRASS ½″, HOOKS – SMALL, HOOKS – LARGE, WASHERS, STRING. There were pots, coils of wire, rolls of string, bags of polythene, bundles of sticks – did he ever throw anything away? Several strings of onions hung from nails in front of the window.

David wound a lever on the work-bench and watched as the two metal jaws of the vice moved together. He slipped his finger in and tightened it till he felt the metal grip.

"No!" he grimaced between clenched teeth. "You won't get anything from me. Martian – Captain, serial number 649321, that's all I'll ever tell you."

"Damn you British!" he answered in a vaguely foreign accent.

He freed his finger and wandered to the deep shelves opposite the window. The larger items were stored here. Some folding chairs, bags of fertilisers, large flower-pots, some old sacks, a bit of old carpet – but as he ran his hand along, it met something rigid and squarish. He lifted up the corner of the carpet and looked under: it was almost too dark to see but he could make out a handle. He tugged at it. It was heavy, but inch by inch it slid forward. A suitcase – quite old, by the look of it, with metal corners. He slid back the catches. Click, they both sprang up. He lifted the lid but the shelf above restricted its movement. Crouching down, he peered in but it was too dark to make out its contents. He slipped in his hand and felt around – his fingers slid between what seemed to be papers and books. He pulled something out – a photo. He took it to the window to examine it.

His own face stared back at him, the hair flopping forward, his own lop-sided grin smiled back. Except that he'd never posed for this photo. It was the same gangly, relaxed posture but he'd never worn those shorts, and he hadn't worn plimsolls since the infants. How could it possibly be him?

Something caught his eye. He looked up. Hurrying towards the shed beneath a large black umbrella was Grandad. Quickly, David shut the case, pushed it back, pulled the carpet and sacking back into place and was just slipping the photo into his jeans pocket when the shed door opened and Grandad said, "There you are. Come on then, lad, let's make some dinner."

Chapter Seven

As soon as he could escape to his room, David ran upstairs, quietly shut the door, and turned on the light. Grandad had kept him busy, first with scrubbing the potatoes, then with chopping the mint. Afterwards, there'd been the three-stage washing-up duty. Then Grandad had found a shred of mint on the saucepan and had made him wash it again.

"Eight out of ten," Grandad had said on the final inspection and David wondered whether it was ever possible to score ten out of ten from Grandad, even nine out of ten.

The photo was curved from where he'd been sitting on it. But there was no mistake. That was definitely his own face staring back at him. It even had the same brown mole on the right cheekbone, but not the long white scar above the eyebrow. There was something else that bothered him about the photo but he couldn't work out what it was. Not yet.

He put on his Walkman to help him think: it always helped when he was doing homework, perhaps it would help him now.

The resemblance was uncanny. He'd been half-hoping that he'd imagined it, that the gloom of the shed had played tricks on his eyes. But there must be some simple explanation. Perhaps he had a cousin somewhere: cousins sometimes resembled one another, didn't they? But he didn't have any cousins. As far as he knew he had no other relatives on Mum's side of the family, apart from Nan and Grandad Robinson. It was odd how little he knew about Mum and her family and that she never talked about it.

Once he'd complained to her about his middle name, Eric. He'd never liked it. She'd become quite cross and had snapped that it was after someone she'd once known. But then she'd clamped up and had shouted at him not to go on when he'd asked who.

And what was this photo doing in a hidden suitcase in the shed? People only hide things that they don't want others to find. What was Grandad trying to hide? Was it anything to do with Mum?

The trouble is, David thought, every question leads to another question. And he had a feeling no one was going to give him any answers, honest ones anyway. After all, Mum had lied about his coming here, hadn't she?

He threw himself down onto the bed. If only Mark were here, at least he'd have someone to talk to. Perhaps he'd ring him later. He could make an excuse to go out and phone from a call-box. The thought made him feel a little better.

He removed his Walkman and wandered into the bathroom and stood in front of the mirror, studying his reflection. He propped the photo onto the shelf and looked at one face and then the other, faster and faster until the images blurred: a double image merged into one.

He slipped the photo into a buttoned-down pocket of his shirt. Suddenly he felt cold. He fetched his sweatshirt and made his way downstairs.

Grandad was dozing in the armchair, the newspaper spread on his lap, the crossword half done and his pen idle on the page. His chin rested on his chest and he snored gently.

David glanced at the shed key, hanging on its hook by the back door, and then at Grandad. More than anything he wanted to have another look in the suitcase that might give some clues to the boy in the photo. But there was no good reason he would be able to give for going out in the rain to a gloomy shed. Anyway, he wanted time to look properly, in a good light and when there was no danger of being interrupted.

David made his way up the hall and stopped outside Nan's room. He didn't want to go in but his curiosity was nagging at him. Perhaps there was a connection between her and the boy in the photo. Perhaps he'd find it in this room. He grasped the door handle and pushed it open. Even with the curtains open and the boxes and bags removed, he could sense the room's heavy misery. He turned on the light: it made no difference. She's dead, he told himself. She's not here. It's just an empty room.

He made himself step inside. The shelves, the cupboard, the mantelpiece were all bare, but there were some things lying on the chest-of-drawers. He crossed the room and picked them up. But these photos in their frames were very old: a young girl standing with her arm round a boy and several more of them and others he did not recognise. He replaced them, backed out, turned off the light, pulled the door shut and breathed a sigh of relief.

He crossed to the front room door opposite and pushed it open. This room held more possibilities. There were some shelves set into the fireplace alcove, a small bookcase and a large sideboard. The sideboard, which had been set out with trifle and bowls and spoons at the funeral tea, now held a display of photos set out on round lacy mats. But on close inspection, there was nothing he hadn't seen before: Mum and Dad on their wedding day, school photos of himself at various ages, and several of Lizzie, from chubby baby to one of her in her angel's costume from last Christmas's nativity play.

He squatted down before the sideboard doors and pulled them open. There was a vague, musty, sweet smell, like old Christmas cake. He scanned the shelves quickly. A pile of neatly folded tablecloths, several large, flat black cases with brass clasps, some delicate-looking cups and saucers and glass bowls, a dish in the shape of a fish, a pile of old boxed games and playing cards . . . and an old shoe box. He pulled it out and lifted the lid – photographs.

"So, there you are," said Grandad.

David jumped up.

"It's all right, keep your hair on – I don't bite.

What you got there then?"

Grandad reached over and took a photo from the top. He didn't have his glasses on and held it at arm's length, peering at it. David could see it clearly. It was a black and white photo of a young woman. She was wearing a summer dress and sitting on a donkey, on a beach somewhere. Long, wavy hair blew around her pretty face as she laughed and waved at the camera. She looked like the girl in the photo in Nan's room.

"Who's that?" asked David.

"That's your nan," said Grandad.

David could not believe that the laughing, pretty woman could have grown into Nan Robinson.

Grandad stood looking at it for a few seconds, then abruptly placed it back into the box, saying, "Put them back now, David, and give me a hand with the tea."

As Grandad shut the door behind them, the camel clock chimed five and the last line of Grandad's Quarter Jack poem leapt into David's head:

'. . . and so will clang when I'm gone.'

The trouble was, David wasn't so sure Nan had gone.

"I'll show you how to chop onions so they don't make you cry," said Grandad, peeling off the skin of a large onion.

"I don't like onions," said David.

Grandad ignored him.

"The trick is to leave cutting the root end till last. That's the most powerful part of the onion."

David watched as he deftly sliced and chopped with the sharp, slender knife.

"Always keep your fingers slightly bent – see? Out of the way of the knife."

He swept the pile of onions to one side of the chopping board.

"Now, let's see you do it."

"I hate onions," said David shoving his hands into his pockets.

Grandad held out an onion. They stared at one another but Grandad's gaze didn't shift. Sulkily, David took the onion and slowly started to peel it. He hated onions. He hated this house and he hated Mum and Dad for sending him here. He wanted to go home, to be sitting with Mark outside the shelter, frying sausages over the fire. But he wasn't due to go home till Sunday. Four whole days to go.

It took ages and he nearly cut himself twice. The slices were too big and Grandad had to chop them again. Now his fingers smelt. But Grandad hadn't finished with him yet: set the table, butter the toast, grate the cheese . . .

"Now," said Grandad as he sprinkled a handful of buttered cubes of toast onto the onion soup and topped it with a spoonful of grated cheese, "help yourself if you want any more."

David glared at the hated soup. O.K. He'd eat it. He'd even pretend to enjoy it. He'd pretend that it was a test of endurance. He wasn't going to be beaten by anything. He was a survivalist.

Grandad had nearly finished his bowl. Holding his breath so that he wouldn't smell it, David took a spoonful of soup and gulped it down. If you swallowed it quickly it didn't have time to reach the taste buds. It was only when he reached the last few spoonfuls that he realised that he liked it. Especially the pieces of crunchy toast with their swirls of melted cheese.

If you shaded in the pale yellow first, then overlaid it with fine lines of red, orange and brown, you could get exactly the right shades to show the rings of Saturn. With careful shading you could make it look three-dimensional.

David sat at the kitchen table, his tongue stuck to the corner of his mouth in concentration.

You had to use good quality crayons and paper, otherwise the pencils went right through. He liked experimenting with getting exactly the right colours: yellow and black together made a very different sort of green than yellow and blue. The trouble was, people at school kept pinching his crayons or returning them broken. On Saturdays he liked to go into The Art and Craft Shop and look at the parades of coloured pencils in their graduated shades of yellows, blues, reds and greens. He loved the smell of them too. He hadn't done any drawing for ages now, not since they'd been working on the camp. He particularly enjoyed working on shadows, how you could make a crater look deep or shallow. How you could give the impression of light with a touch of highlighting or rubbing away the crayon to show the white paper beneath, or to give a shine to an astronaut's helmet. And he could think while he was doing it about the boy in the photo.

It had stopped raining at last and Grandad was just returning from the compost heap with the empty bucket in his hand, when the phone rang from the hall. It must be Mum, she always rang about this time, thought David. But when David picked up the phone a voice said,

"It's me."

"Mark? Wow! How's things?"

"O.K."

"How's the shelter after all that rain – did it leak or anything?"

"Dunno – haven't looked. I've been busy."

"What?"

"Dad's booked us a holiday – we're leaving in the morning."

"You'll be there when I get back, though?"

"Well, that's why I'm ringing – we'll be gone for ten days."

"Oh, thanks a lot."

"Look, don't blame me. It's not my fault – if you hadn't gone away this probably wouldn't have happened."

"Yes, well, O.K."

David could not disguise the disappointment in his voice.

"I'll send you a postcard."

"Yeh, thanks. Have a good time."

As he put the phone back he remembered the boy in the photo. He wouldn't be able to ask Mark now. He'd never felt quite so alone and miserable.

Grandad was standing at the table, slowly turning the pages of David's drawing book, examining each page closely. He looked at David as he entered, but didn't say a word, just closed it and slid it back to where David had been sitting. Eva would have said something like, "I wish I could draw like that," or "How do you make the shadows look so real, David?" But Grandad just walked out into the garden, down the path towards the shed.

About half an hour later he returned and fetched an old Scrabble game from the sideboard, but it was a waste of time. Grandad spoke very little apart from announcing the score and "Your turn, David," and David could not help brooding about the photo and Mark and the shelter and all the work that had gone in to it: all for nothing.

As he lay in bed later, trying to rewind the tape of the day's events in his head, it was as if he was watching someone else. He was not in control any more: events were taking him over. He felt like a character in a film or a story, and he could only play the part that had been written for him. Someone knew what was going on, but it wasn't him.

Chapter Eight

He was travelling on a coach, but instead of the usual coach seats, everyone was sitting in soft, pink, velvet armchairs around coffee tables, like Auntie Bird's. Nan Robinson was driving the coach, grimly hanging onto the wheel and glaring ahead. Auntie Bird was making her way down the coach, handing out chocolate cake and drinks, but every time the coach swerved, chairs went skidding and drinks and cake went flying in all directions. Grandad and Mark were sitting opposite, chatting away to each other. Mark kept picking up pieces of cake, gulping them down and saying 'waste not, want not'.

"I didn't realise you knew Mark," David said to Grandad. "This used to be Mark," Grandad replied. "But now he's Napoleon."

"No, he's not. I am!" yelled Nan from the driving seat.

Although he couldn't see them, David knew that somewhere, at the back of the coach, were his parents, watching him. Everyone in the coach appeared to know where it was going, but every time he asked, they ignored him.

When he opened his eyes, it took David a few minutes to orientate himself, to separate reality from his dream. His mind was still crowded with the images. He didn't dream very often, but when he did, they were usually extraordinary.

The dream left him feeling unsettled and slightly depressed. Even as he dressed he couldn't shake off the feeling.

He was just finishing washing up the breakfast things when the front doorbell rang. Grandad called, "Someone for you, David."

A girl was waiting on the path, sitting astride her bike, arms folded impatiently. She was rather plump with thick, curly red hair and freckles, wearing shorts that showed thin legs, and a baggy tee-shirt emblazoned with the message HANDS OFF ANTARCTICA around a picture of two penguins.

"My Aunt Jess sent me," she said, gesturing with her head towards Auntie Bird's house next door.

She looked as pleased about her being sent as David did.

"Right," he said.

"What d'you want to do then?"

He shrugged. He supposed this must be Hannah. He searched in his mind for some excuse to send her away. The last thing he wanted was to be paired up with some girl. He had enough problems already. He wanted time to think, to plan how to get another look at the suitcase, and time to feel sorry for himself.

Grandad appeared behind him.

"It's going to be a nice day," he said. "Come along then, David, you can borrow my bike."

Moodily, David followed Grandad round to the side of the house, where behind a bush an old wooden shed leaned against the wall. Taking a bunch of keys from his pocket, he unlocked the padlock, opened the door and pulled out his bike. It was a huge, heavy, black, old-fashioned thing with a large shopping basket on the front.

"Hop on then – try it for size. Mmmm, hold on a jif."

He disappeared into the shed and re-appeared with a spanner in his hand.

"Now, try again," he said after he'd lowered the seat and the handlebars. "Just the job. Good old bike that, bought it in '49."

Without a word, Hannah turned and was out of the gate and pedalling down the road. By the time he'd mounted the bike she had already turned the corner. He manoeuvred the heavy frame out of the gate, thinking it was a good job none of his friends could see him now. He'd never live it down.

"Dinner's at twelve," called Grandad.

He had to pedal hard to keep up. Grandad's bike only had three gears and Hannah's racer could easily outpace him. Suddenly she stopped, leant the bike against the street lamp, and started to rummage in the litter bin attached to it. As he drew up behind her, she threw a couple of drink cans into her pannier and without a word, pedalled off again, only to repeat the performance at the next litter bin. After half an hour, David realised they weren't going anywhere. They had come full-circle, with a few detours for side streets, stopping at every litter bin on the way.

As she turned into the riverside car park, David made a supreme effort, overtaking her and forcing her to swerve and brake. He grabbed her handlebars.

"You idiot!" she yelled.

"Look, I've had enough of this Visitors' Guide To the Litter Bins of Wimborne. What are you playing at? If this is your idea of a joke, I'm going."

"Collecting aluminium is not a joke!" she said crossly. "Do you know how many cans are thrown away every year in Britain?"

She didn't wait for an answer.

"Nearly five million. And do you know how much is recycled? Five per cent – that's all. In Sweden they recycle ninety-five per cent!"

"What are you going on about?"

She sighed and pointed to a large metal container across the car park, labelled ALUMINIUM CANS ONLY.

He followed her and watched her take the cans from her panniers and start to jump on them.

"Go on," she said. "They have to be flattened first."
He laid down the bike and started to stamp on the cans.

As they were feeding the last of the cans into the container, Hannah muttered, "Oh no, not the Barbie Twins."

David looked up to see two girls in tight leggings, short suntops and bright pink trainers walking along the river path towards them.

"Hiya, Hannah," called one with long cascading curly hair. "Saving the world are we?"

The other one, with a pony-tail, giggled.

"You didn't tell us you had a boyfriend," said the pony-tail.

David felt himself colour slightly.

"He doesn't look your sort – too thin for you I'd say." She nudged her friend and they giggled.

David picked up his bike.

"Wow, take a look at that – it must weigh a ton."

"Looks as if he's got the same taste in bikes as in girls," said the long-haired one.

Hannah eyed them shrewdly, letting them have their say. Then she said, "He doesn't understand English. He's French. The bike's on loan from a neighbour while he's here on holiday. His dad's a record producer, working in London this week. I'm showing him around."

"Yeh, I bet," said the pony-tail.

"Go on, then. Ask him."

Then suddenly they went coy, looking at one another.

"Go on, you ask him."

"No, you."

"All right then. Is your dad a record producer?"

"*Ah, oui,*" said David, searching his memory for the French phrases Miss Elliot had struggled to teach him.

The two girls eyed him suspiciously.

"Go on then, ask him to say something in French," said the long-haired one to Hannah.

"O.K." She turned to David.

"*André, est-ce-que tu peux me dire quelquechose en français pour mes amies, s'il tu plait?*"

David didn't understand much of it, but he knew what she was getting at.

"*Ah, oui,*" he mumbled.

Perhaps if he threw in everything he could remember and said it very quickly . . .

"*Je m'appelle – André – il fait beau aujourd hui – le gare est prés d'ici – ma soeur a six ans – il pleut – je me lève a sept heurs – et j'aime les frîtes.*"

The two girls looked impressed.

"What did he say?" the pony-tail asked Hannah.

"He says he likes it here and you are both very pretty," she lied.

The two girls smiled at one another.

"Anyway, we've got to go – André?" said Hannah mounting her bike.

They pedalled away as the two girls giggled and waved.

"Where are we going?" called David as they cycled along a long straight tree-lined road.

"Badbury Rings."

"Where?"

"It's the remains of an Iron Age hill fort. We're nearly there."

They climbed to the top of the hill, scaling the earth ramparts that encircled it.

"I thought you said there was a fort," said David as they reached the top, disappointed to find just clumps of trees and shrubs.

"I said remains. Look, see those breaks in the ramparts, that's where the Romans cut through after they'd demolished the settlement – so they could march straight through."

They sat at the top, looking down on the ribbon of road that they'd cycled along. The wind blew David's hair over his eyes and he pushed it back.

"You ought to use gel on that," said Hannah.

"Get lost."

"It would stop it flopping about."

"Yeh, well perhaps you could use some on your tongue – that flops about too much."

She grinned. "Hey, that's quite funny, for a boy. Anyway, I hate gel. All the boys who use it are right posers."

David wondered whether he should feel flattered. He couldn't make up his mind either, about whether he felt cross about the games she'd played on him or whether he admired her cheek.

"I often come up here," she said, sweeping her arm in a dramatic gesture. "Far from the madding crowd."

David screwed up his face. "Do what?"

"It's the title of a book by Thomas Hardy."

David leaned back on his elbows and taking a deep breath recited:

> "The Jack o'clock never forgets;
> Ding dong;

Just so did he clang before I came
And so will clang when I'm gone."

"What are you going on about?" said Hannah.

"It's a poem by Thomas Hardy. Fancy you not knowing that."

He lay back feeling very pleased with himself.

Suddenly Hannah burst out laughing.

"Did you see their faces? All that gibberish you were waffling and they were completely gob-smacked. Just shows how stupid they are. You did very well, considering you were talking total rubbish."

"How come you speak French then?"

"I did an exchange this year. Personally I can't see what everyone finds so difficult."

They lay on their backs, stretched out beneath a clear, blue sky. As David squinted away from the sun, a kite, in the shape of a bird, hovered in the distance, swooping occasionally as its invisible owner tugged a string. As he rolled onto his front, he remembered the photo inside his shirt pocket. He took it out. Hannah, peering at him through half-closed eyes sat up and leant over to have a look.

"What did they cut your hair with?" she asked. "A bread knife?"

"What?"

He looked more closely. She had a point: the hair of the boy in the photo was very slightly different and more bushy at the sides.

"Anyway, it's not me," he said.

"Let's have a proper look then."

She peered at it closely.

"It's got to be you. Look, there's your mole."

"Look," he said, pointing to his scar, "I've had this since . . . well, since I can remember. He hasn't got one."

She looked from one to the other, comparing David's face with the photo.

"Who is it then?"

"I don't know."

"How come you've got the photo then, if you don't know who he is?"

"I found it in Grandad's shed – in a suitcase. There's loads more stuff inside but I didn't have time to get a proper look."

"Let's have another look . . . wow! It's amazing, it's so much like you. I know, perhaps it's your *doppel-gänger*."

"My what?"

"Your *doppel-gänger* . . . it's your spirit and if it appears to its living owner it means you're going to die very soon."

"Oh, thanks a lot."

"But I don't think you can photograph *doppel-gängers*."

She studied the photo closely.

"I suppose it's possible that you could have a double somewhere but then it's not very likely that your grandad would have a photo of him. I know! You must have an identical twin."

"Don't be daft," said David, snatching the photo

back. "I'd know, wouldn't I?"

Hannah sat up and clasped her knees. She was getting quite excited.

"Not necessarily," she said. "It's happened before, twins being separated at birth and only discovering it years later. I read about it in one of Mum's magazines. There were these twin sisters, quite old, about forty, and one of them found out and traced the other one. They both said that they'd always felt part of them was missing and when they met up, it was like being complete again. But the amazing thing was they'd both called their children by the same names, even had the same sort of dog. Hey, you haven't ever felt part of you was missing, have you?"

"Yeh, I'm missing out on the camp I had planned with my friend Mark, but thanks to Mum, I'm stuck here with Grandad instead."

"What?" said Hannah.

"Never mind," said David with a heavy sigh.

"Right, let's think," said Hannah, rocking backwards and forwards in concentration. "If you really are a twin, there are several possibilities. Either your mother kept you and had your twin adopted, *or* your mother had you adopted and kept the twin *or* your real mother had you both adopted, which means your mum may not be your real mother at all, or your father, come to that."

"It's too stupid," said David. "Even if it were true, they'd have told me, wouldn't they? Lots of kids are adopted but it's no great secret."

He put the photo back into his shirt and stretched out on the grass. It hadn't been a good idea, letting Hannah see the photo. It had triggered more questions and doubts in his head.

"Hey, this is really exciting," said Hannah, undeterred. "I've always wondered whether I'm adopted. It would explain everything."

"What, like you're secretly a princess?" said David.

"Don't be stupid," she sneered contemptuously.

David almost flinched.

She threw herself down and leaned on her elbows.

"That's a typical sexist remark. The fact is, I have nothing whatsoever in common with any of my family."

David thought Hannah's appearance had a lot in common with Auntie Bird's but thought that perhaps it was not a good idea to say so.

"For example," she continued. "Do you know what my mother spent a whole two weeks doing? Seeing how many things she could fit into a matchbox."

"What for?" asked David.

"Oh, some daft competition at T.G. or something. Can you believe that? The hole in the ozone getting bigger and bigger, two thirds of the world starving, the rain-forests going up in smoke and my mother is searching for things to fit into a matchbox. And what's worse, she won and got her photo in *The Evening Echo*. It was *so* embarrassing."

She cupped her hands over her eyes and squinted

into the sky towards the kite.

"Anyway," she said, without looking at David, "why don't you just ask your grandad?"

"I can't – there's something funny about it – the way it's all hidden away. I've got a feeling I'm not meant to know. And he's not exactly the easiest person to talk to, either."

"Well, you'll have to take another look inside the case – you might discover who he is."

"It's not that simple. Grandad's either working inside the shed or not far away. He'd notice if I was poking around, and he's hardly ever out of the garden."

"We've just got to think of a good reason to spend time in the shed, so that we can grab the chance to look. He has to go indoors some time."

"Yeh, but I'm usually with him, scraping the potatoes or doing stage three of the washing-up."

"What?"

"Forget it."

David wasn't sure about whether he wanted Hannah interfering.

"I'll think of something," said Hannah.

But David had already thought of something. And although he resented her "*We* can grab the chance to look", he could see that she might prove useful.

Chapter Nine

Grandad had dinner ready and waiting.

"Is it all right if Hannah comes round this afternoon?" asked David, trying to sound casual and keeping his eyes focused on his potato salad.

"We thought we might make a kite then fly it at Badbury Rings."

Grandad looked slightly surprised.

"Well, I need to do some work on the apple trees, but if you can wait a bit, I'll give you a hand," he said.

"No, it's O.K. – we can do it ourselves," said David hurriedly, still avoiding Grandad's eye. "I've made one before – in C.D.T. at school. It's dead easy. If we could just have a few plant sticks and some polythene, we'll be fine. Hannah will bring the rest. It was her idea," he added quickly, "but her mum's a bit fussy about glue and paints and things in the house – we thought perhaps we could use the shed."

"Well, as long as you leave everything as you find it."

Hannah turned up later with a carrier bag containing an old kite reel of her brother's and other things that she thought might come in useful, including a stapler and a very professional-looking pair of scissors.

"Mum'll kill me if she knows," said Hannah. "They're her dressmaking scissors. But she's out this afternoon, so she won't notice."

They wandered down to the shed and Grandad came over.

"Plant sticks here, polythene over there, stanley knife up there, wire cutters, anything else you need, just ask. I better show you how this works," he said, reaching for the stanley knife.

"It's all right, Grandad," insisted David. "I've used them at school. Always cut away from you, fingers out of the way, all that sort of thing."

"You're very E.F., Mr Robinson," announced Hannah who had been gazing round the shed.

"E.F.?" said Grandad.

"Environmentally friendly," informed Hannah. "You know, recycling things."

"Well, good," said Grandad and returned to his trees.

"Where is it?" muttered Hannah, when he had gone.

"Behind you," said David, gesturing with his head. "On the shelves underneath that sacking."

They didn't say much for a while, being mainly pre-occupied with watching Grandad's progress around the garden, trying to gauge an opportunity to make a grab at the suitcase.

"Hey, slow down a bit," said Hannah suddenly. "You'll have finished before we've had a chance to look. You should have gone for something more complex, like a hexagon. Diamond-shaped kites are very conventional. Hey, don't cut it that close – you won't have enough margin to fold it over."

"Look, am I doing this or are you?" he demanded.

"It's supposed to be both of us," said Hannah. "But you just carry on. I'll do the creative bit, the painting."

She heaved herself onto the workbench and picked at the end of the sellotape.

"I wonder what his name is," she said.

"Who?"

"Your twin."

"You've got twins on the brain," said David.

"Yes, but just imagine if I'm right – it could mean that one or both of your parents aren't your real parents at all."

"I'd got that far. Look hold this down while I staple it in place."

"No. You hold it down while I staple it in place," she said grabbing the stapler. "It would mean," she continued, "that you'd have to discover your real parents for the first time. And you might have brothers and sisters that you never . . ."

She stopped in mid-sentence and smiled at the doorway. "It's going really well, Mr Robinson."

"Just going to pop these beetroots round to Jess next door," said Grandad.

They stared at one another, stood motionless as he made his way up the path and as soon as he was out of sight, they raced to the shelf, pulled away the sacking and carpet, tugged at the handle of the suitcase and released the catches.

"Quick!" said David. "Hold the lid up for me."

He'd been right. In sunlight, although his view was still restricted, he could clearly make out the bulging contents of photos, papers and envelopes. He grabbed a fat, manilla envelope and a handful of photos.

"Quick," said Hannah, "drop them in here."

She held open the carrier bag. David shoved the suitcase back.

"We'll do it in stages," he said. "Unless we can be sure of enough time to get it right out. Give it here."

Hannah was already peering inside the bag and it wasn't right that she should have the first look. He lifted out the envelope and shook it, but it was so tightly packed that he had to pull at the contents.

They were school photos: black and white school photos. Some were still in their smart cardboard frames, grey, brown, maroon: several embossed with gold patterns. David stared.

"It's him, isn't it?" said Hannah. "He must be about five in this one. Look at his chubby little hands."

A round-faced boy with neatly parted, shiny hair, sat proudly in striped tie, and sleeveless grey jumper, grey-sleeved arms folded tightly over his chest, with a book open on the table in front of him.

Hannah turned it upside down.

"Look, you can even read the words:

'Play! Play! Play! Play Billy!
Billy can play.
See Billy play.'

Wow!" said Hannah. "It's really exciting. I wonder how it ended?"

But David was not listening. He was studying the other photos. They lay there in their stiff frames, showing a boy in the growing stages of school life: in grey shirts, white shirts, knitted jumpers, blazers, ties with tie pins and without, but always smiling, as if school was every boy's dream come true. The neatly combed hair was only in evidence in a few photos, giving way to the flopping fringe that David knew so well.

"Did you look like this?" asked Hannah.

"I think so," said David. "Except for the parting in the hair."

"They look a bit old-fashioned, don't they?" said Hannah. "School photos don't look like this any more. They're always in colour for a start. These look yonks old."

"So much for your twin theory," said David.

"Mmm," said Hannah wrinkling her nose in disappointment. "Shame. Hey – watch out, he's coming back."

They scooped them back into the carrier.

"We can take them back to my house," she whispered. "They're all out. We could say we've forgotten something."

Grandad had stopped on the path to dead-head some roses.

"Come on, then," said Hannah, grabbing the bag.

David followed her out, frowning with irritation.

"We need some special glue," Hannah was saying. "But I think we've got some at home. We're just going to fetch it."

Grandad glanced at David with curiosity, then nodded. Suddenly, David felt the need to assert himself with this bossy girl. He ran past her to the gate, then shouted, "Well, are you coming or not?"

He couldn't quite decide whether she really needed to re-tie her shoe lace at that moment, or whether it was just one of her little games.

David could detect the lingering trace of air freshener as he stepped through the front door of Hannah's house. The sunlight bounced off shiny horse brasses, warming pans, trays and plates that covered every surface. A huge light-hanging that made David think of an octopus dominated the tiny hall. He moved round it cautiously.

"Awful, isn't it?" said Hannah. "Look, these aren't even real." She grabbed a large rose from an elaborate flower arrangement and crushed and twisted it viciously. She released it and it sprang back to perfection.

She led the way upstairs.

"That's my brother's," she sneered. David looked admiringly at a life-size poster stuck to a door, showing a snarling commando aiming a machine gun.

"You can see what I have to put up with," she added. "Fortunately he's away on cadet camp at the moment." David felt a twinge of envy.

"This is my room," she announced proudly.

On the door, stuck to an old shaving mirror, was a label saying THE GREATEST THREAT TO PLANET EARTH, and a large sign announcing PEOPLE OF A NERVOUS DISPOSITION SHOULD NOT ENTER THIS ROOM. Someone had crossed out NERVOUS and inserted NORMAL.

Once through the door, for a brief moment David forgot about the bag and its photos. He was too engrossed in studying the walls.

"That's my 'Wall of Horrors'," explained Hannah.

"Ugh," grimaced David. "What do you want those on your wall for?"

"They're a constant reminder of man's inhumanity to animals," said Hannah.

"What's this one?" he asked, curling his lip in distaste.

"That's a rabbit that's been used for experiments, that's a fox rescued from a pack of hounds, those are dolphins entangled in a drift net, that's a battery hen after . . ."

"I think I get the message," said David.

"And this is my campaign wall," she smiled.

'Dear Miss Gilmour,' David read,

'We regret to learn that you will no longer be purchasing our Lash-Glo mascara. However, we can assure you that our policy on animal testing states that . . .'

There were lots more letters of a similar nature. The other walls were covered with posters urging the readers to save the rain-forest, and warning about threats to whales, seals, dolphins and the planet in general. David felt quite overwhelmed by it all.

"You ought to meet Eva," he said after a while. "That's my other gran. She's vegetarian."

"Really?" said Hannah, sounding totally unimpressed.

He knelt onto the carpet and tipped out the photos.

"Hey, there are dates written on the backs," said Hannah. "Summer 1964, July 1962, Eric 1959 . . ."

"Let me see that," demanded David.

It was the photo of the chubby boy with the reading book. 'Eric 1959' was pencilled clearly on the back.

"Most of them are dated on the backs," said Hannah, sorting them into order. "There's one here of a football team, and a class photo too. They go up to 1965."

"My middle name's Eric," said David.

"Is it?" cried Hannah, suddenly interested. "That has to be a major clue. Do you know why?"

"No," said David. "I asked Mum once but all she would say was that it was after someone she knew. She got a bit ratty when I pushed it."

Hannah's face took on the look of someone who had just discovered a dead body in the wardrobe.

"What are you looking like that for?" he asked.

"Don't you see – someone she once knew? Your mother named you after him? Even the dates fit. Look, if he was, say five, in 1959, that means he was born about 1954, which would make him . . ."

"Thirty-seven," said David.

"Old enough," continued Hannah, "to be your . . ."

". . . father?" finished David.

Hannah nodded.

David leaned back, tongue stuck to the corner of his mouth in concentration.

"Let's look at all the other photos first, before we start leaping to conclusions."

Hannah sighed with impatience.

They spread them all out. They were all black and white, many of baby Eric: sitting up in large pram with a woolly hat, or lying on a rug, astride a rocking-horse or in a playpen. There was one of a cub camp where they picked him out from a line of boys, holding mugs and plates. Hannah picked out one of a chubby toddler on a tricycle.

"That's the rec., I'm certain," she said. "Look, you can see the houses in Redcott Road. Well, he must have lived in Wimborne. That's another clue."

There was one of him as a toddler, seated on an armchair, tightly clasping a small baby, another on a beach with a little girl, patting sandcastles, and another of two heavily muffled children in balaclavas sitting astride a sledge in the snow. And there were several others of the older Eric, David's look-alike. One of him on a bike and another of him peering out of a tent with two other boys.

They also found an eight-of-spades and a three-of-hearts from a pack of playing cards, a label that said 'to Eric, lots of love, Mum and Dad' and some cartoon cards that had come out of sweet cigarette packets.

David scanned them slowly, turning them over for clues. 'Swanage 1958' said one, 'Eric aged eighteen months', 'Big brother' and 'Brrrr! It's cold'.

Hannah fetched a notepad and pencil.

"Right," she said, "let's see what we know."

She printed the word FACTS and underlined it. Then she wrote: Name Eric

D.O.B. 1954 ??

"That makes him about thirty-seven," said David. She wrote: 'Approx age 37

'Probably lived in Wimborne', she added.

She chewed her pencil. "Anything else?"

"Well, it may not mean anything . . ." said David.

"Go on!"

"Well, it was something I overheard a woman say at the funeral. She said that I looked just like someone, that I was the image of . . . but she didn't finish what she was saying. When she saw me, she stopped and changed the subject."

"It's a major clue," said Hannah.

She got busy with her pencil again and wrote the heading THE FATHER THEORY

Evidence

1. the name Eric
2. the dates
3. the overheard
4. David looks like the boy Eric
5. mother once knew someone called Eric.

David leaned back and drew up his knees.

"It all fits," declared Hannah. "It's perfect!"

"Yes, but . . ."

Hannah tossed the pad down. "Well you come up with a better explanation!"

"O.K.," said David. "Let's say it's true. Why would Mum have kept it a secret? If Dad is really my stepfather, that's not so terrible, is it? Loads of kids have stepfathers."

"When were your parents married?" asked Hannah, narrowing her eyes.

"How should I know?"

Hannah sat resting her chin on her hands, deep in thought.

"I know!" she cried. "She was married to Eric before your dad, but he turned out to be a criminal or something and they've decided to keep it a secret in case it ruined your life."

David made a face. The one of weary impatience that he had perfected for Warren.

"Then why would she have all his photos and stuff in the shed? No, it doesn't fit together."

David didn't want it to fit together. He was beginning to resent this Eric. He was an intruder. He suddenly felt very protective of Dad: his bald patch, his courage in facing up to Norman Stebbings, his funny stories from school. He didn't want another father.

"He could have died young, and she inherited all his possessions," suggested Hannah.

David sighed and nodded in mock agreement.

"Yeh, including half a million pounds in unused bank notes at the bottom of the suitcase."

"You have to consider all possibilities," insisted Hannah, doodling on her pad. "It's called lateral thinking."

"Have you got somewhere safe to keep these?" asked David, as he piled up the photos.

Hannah lifted off a box file from her shelf labelled ENDANGERED SPECIES, slid them in, and snapped it shut.

"Tomorrow," he said, "whatever happens, I'm going to have another look."

When they got back, Grandad was in the shed, cleaning up his tools, so they decided to leave the kite till the next day. It was nearly teatime anyway and Hannah was expected by her Aunt Jess.

After she had gone, Grandad poked his head out from the shed. "Auntie Bird's arranged a nice surprise for tomorrow," he called. "She's taking us all to Studland for the day, Hannah too. So, I'll need you to give me a hand this evening. Everything's going to need a good watering."

Later, just as David was struggling down to the greenhouse with a can of water, Hannah turned up.

"Mum's gone mad," she announced. "I left her scissors in your shed."

She followed him into the greenhouse.

"Did you know about tomorrow? Studland?" she muttered.

"Mmmm," hummed David moodily.

"I thought I might make an excuse not to go, then sneak down to the shed when you'd all gone," she whispered.

"Well, you can't because he keeps it locked. Anyway, it's not your suitcase. It's nothing to do with you. If anyone opens it, it's going to be me. I decide what to do. Got it?"

"No need to get so macho," hissed Hannah.

She fetched her scissors and he watched the whale on the back of her tee-shirt shrink to a tadpole as she stomped up towards the gate.

Chapter Ten

David sat in the back of Auntie Bird's car next to Hannah, struggling not to topple onto her as they swerved round a corner.

It was not yet eight o'clock by the time they reached the Sandbanks car ferry that would take them to Studland Bay. David had learned in the course of the journey, how much Auntie Bird hated traffic queues and felt he could answer any questions, without having to 'pass' once, on the subject of *Traffic Jams I Have Known* by Mrs J. Bird.

"There'll be a queue here a mile long by nine o'clock," Auntie Bird predicted cheerfully as they sat watching the ferry float slowly towards them from the other side of the bay.

"What's that noise?" asked David.

"It's the chains," said Hannah. "The ferry pulls itself along chains slung between Sandbanks and Studland."

Once they'd driven onto the ferry, she and David left the car and stood leaning over the rail, along with several backpackers and small excited children who were clutching buckets and spades. The ferry slowly clanked its way across the gently rippling water.

Already the sun was hot and the day seemed to be

coloured with the cleanest blues and palest yellows. David could not imagine why he had not wanted to come.

As they trod over the warm sand, David could see that, apart from a handful of scattered families, the beach stretched uncluttered into the distance and to their right rippled soft curving dunes. But already the sea was bobbing with heads, and dinghies and lilos.

Auntie Bird gave orders, and soon they had requisitioned their territory, with rugs, deckchairs, windbreaks, a huge umbrella, and a line of bags and picnic boxes forming a rear-guard defence.

"Once the holiday-makers descend," she said, "you're lucky if you have room to swing a cat."

He half-expected Hannah to denounce the swinging of cats but she did not appear to have heard, being busy with unfolding a dinghy from a hold-all.

"Just look at that!" demanded Auntie Bird.

They all looked.

"Can you credit it? Some people think the beach belongs to them."

They watched her plod down to a group of youths who had just jumped from a motor-boat and were pulling it onto the beach directly in line with their view of the sea. After much arm-waving from Auntie Bird they eventually pushed it further along, just in front of another family who had spent ten minutes settling themselves in place.

Grandad chose to ignore it all. He sat comfortably in

his deckchair, a straw hat on his head, trousers rolled up and newspaper on his lap.

"Who's coming in with me then?" demanded Auntie Bird when she returned.

"I need some help with this first," said Hannah.

She had been pumping away for five minutes on the foot pump, but the dinghy looked as if it hadn't noticed.

"Let's have a go then," David offered, leaping up.

"I'm thirsty," said Hannah, relinquishing the pump.

"There's squash in the brown picnic box," instructed Auntie Bird. "Help yourself. I'm going to change."

Auntie Bird disappeared into something that resembled an enormous shoe-bag which gathered at the neck with a drawstring, and she started to change. Immediately the song 'there was an old woman who swallowed a fly' sprang into David's head and he watched the bag shake and wobble as she gyrated out of her clothes and into her costume, expecting that at any moment, fly, spider, bird, cat, dog, cow and horse would come galloping out.

The big mistake was catching Hannah's eye, and the pained expression on his face as he struggled to contain his giggles made Hannah shoot out a mouthful of squash all over the rug.

"Hannah!" reprimanded Auntie Bird.

Hannah and David lay at opposite ends of the dinghy, eyes closed, resting their heads on the fat pillow of the rim.

"I wonder if it's lunchtime yet," said Hannah sleepily.

David pushed the wet hair out of his eyes.

"Did you know my Nan Robinson?" he asked.

"No."

"But you must have seen something of her, with your Aunt Jess living next door."

"I don't think she ever went out, did she? Wasn't she a bit weird?"

"What d'you mean, weird?"

"I don't know – it's only what I heard."

"Why, what did they say then?"

"Nothing! All I know is that Aunt Jess used to spend a lot of time there. She used to sort of baby-sit or something."

"Baby-sit?"

"You know what I mean – keep an eye on her when your grandad was out. Anyway, you should know. She was your grandmother."

"Not really. I hadn't seen her since I was five – or Grandad."

Hannah opened her eyes.

"What, you never came to visit or anything?"

"Nope. Mum did though. She was always going off."

"Was she?" said Hannah, suddenly sitting upright.

She waited for David to respond, but he just lay there, eyes closed, trailing a loose hand in the water.

She leant over and splashed water into his face.

"Oi!" he shouted, shaking himself up. "Right, two can play at that game!"

But before he had the chance she had rolled the boat over, tipping them both into the water.

As he bobbed up, she said,

"You know what I think? I think your mum came to visit on her own so that she could see Eric."

As they dragged the dinghy up the beach they could see that Auntie Bird was setting out plastic plates and mugs onto a tablecloth.

"Cor, great!" said David as they lowered the boat. "I didn't know you'd brought binoculars. Can I have a look?"

Grandad removed the strap from his neck and passed them to David.

"It's amazing," said David, "you can see the people in the sea, just as if they were only a few feet away."

Auntie Bird gave Grandad a long slow look and said, "That's what they're for."

In order to avoid queues at the ferry, they drove a different route home. Corfe Castle beckoned at them from miles away: towering in the distance like a broken crown on a huge, sloping head. As they followed the road that wound past its steep mound, Grandad started to tell them stories about it which lasted most of the way home: of murdered kings, and wicked queens, of prisoners starving in dungeons, of Civil War and betrayals.

David noticed Hannah's rapt expression and felt a sense of discomfort: Grandad wasn't such a bad sort:

now that he was getting used to his ways and routines. When you least expected it, he'd surprise you. And David was a small child again, sitting on Grandad's knee and falling into the ditch and they were both laughing. Did he really remember that, or had he imagined it? It would be good to see Grandad laugh again.

". . . so when King John heard that the hermit had prophesied his downfall, he had him dragged all the way to Wareham behind a horse, where they slung up his bleeding, broken body for everyone to see."

Blow, thought David. I've missed a good bit.

David was in the garden, shaking the sand out of his trainers when Hannah's red hair popped up at the fence.

"Quick, quick!" she yelled. "Blossom's had her kittens," and then she was gone.

Hannah met him in Auntie Bird's kitchen. She put her finger to her lips and stepped carefully out to the hall where Auntie Bird was crouching down and peering into the understairs cupboard. She swapped places with David so that he could have a look.

Blossom, still huge it seemed to David, lay stretched out in a long, cut-down cardboard box. She was licking vigorously at a tiny, wet kitten. Another was pummelling and suckling at her fluffy underside, but another lay weakly beside it.

"I'm a bit concerned about that little one," Auntie Bird whispered. "He should be suckling by now."

The kitten that was being licked crawled to join the other one, where it was soon pummelling and suckling too.

Blossom turned toward the motionless kitten, pulled it towards her with her mouth and started to lick energetically. It made a tiny movement.

"Come on," Auntie Bird said. "Best leave them alone for a bit."

"Has she had them all?" asked Hannah.

"I think so," said Auntie Bird, "but I'm no expert. I'm only going by the book I got from the pet shop. I've never had kittens before."

"What about the little one?" asked David. "Will it be all right?"

"We'll have to wait and see. Apparently, all that licking gets them breathing properly. Though what I'm going to do with three kittens, goodness knows. And it couldn't have happened at a more inconvenient time – I've got the church fête on Saturday."

Chapter Eleven

"It's going to be another scorcher," observed Grandad on Friday morning, as he stood at the back door looking down the garden. "This hose-pipe ban is a blessed nuisance."

"Wimborne Market today," he announced turning to David who was still eating his porridge. "I'm wanting some lettuce seeds, so you can come along with me. You'll like it there – lots of interesting stalls."

"Can't I stay and get on with the kite?" asked David. "There's only today and tomorrow – I'm going home on Sunday."

Grandad looked at him as if he could read his mind. Was it possible that he could see the suitcase spot-lighted in his thoughts?

"Plenty of time for that when we get back," assured Grandad. "I'm responsible for you while you're here. What would your mum say if I left you on your own with sharp knives and the like?"

There was a tap on the kitchen window and Hannah's round, freckled face squinted in. She appeared at the back door, astride her bike.

"Aunt Jess has asked me to keep an eye on the kittens," she informed them. "You ought to see them now – they're all fluffy." She looked at Grandad. "She said to tell you that if you want a lift to the market, she's leaving in ten minutes."

"Get a move on then, David," urged Grandad.

"Can't I go and see the kittens instead? Please, Grandad."

Grandad hesitated for a moment. "Well, I don't see why not, but you'd better check with Jess first."

"Blossom hasn't left them yet," said Hannah. "Not once. Aunt Jess has to bring all her food to her and she's had to give her a litter tray. She has to be fed frequently to keep her strength up. I've got to feed her again at about ten."

The three kittens had changed from sad, wet rags to three balls of fluffy fur: one grey, one tortoiseshell and the tiniest one was black with a white nose and white socks. He was suckling while the other two lay asleep.

"He always waits till the other two have finished," observed Hannah.

"How do you know it's a 'he'?" said David.

"I bet it is."

David stood up from his kneeling position.

"How long will they be at the market?"

"Don't know," said Hannah. "Depends – an hour at least. Why?"

David slipped his hand into his pocket and dangled a large key.

"To the shed," he said.

Now that they had dragged the suitcase out and laid it

on the work-bench, David could only stare at it. He could almost see himself, from a distance, immobilised. His impatience and curiosity had given way to anxious uncertainty.

"Go on!" urged Hannah. "What are you waiting for? Open it!"

He flicked the catches and lifted the lid.

"What if they come back?" he said.

"They won't," said Hannah with impatience.

He didn't know where to begin. Envelopes, packets, folders, photos, books, odd bits of paper overlapped one another. He wanted to tip it out, rifle through it, searching till he found one thing that told him who Eric was. But would he recognise it, even if he found it?

Hannah was watching him. "Look," she said, "we've got to be systematic. Put the photos here . . ." she tapped the corner of the work-bench, "odd bits here, folders and envelopes there . . ."

She started to sort through.

"There's some books here," said David, digging beneath the layers of papers, "and some comics – *Eagle*, *Victor*, *Beano*. And there's a game – 'Owzat', and another box – Meccano! But it doesn't tell us anything we don't already know."

"Hey, look at this," said Hannah, picking out another black and white photo. "Isn't this your grandad?"

David snatched the photo from her. The boy Eric was holding a younger girl while she balanced, donkey-ride style, on a smiling woman kneeling on the grass. Standing behind them, as Hannah said, was a man who David was certain was a younger version of Grandad, with thick dark hair. And the smiling woman was the same as the one in the shoe box photo. It was Nan Robinson.

"It was taken in this garden," said David. "But look – there's no fence at the bottom. I knew there was something odd about the first photo I found of Eric. It was in this garden, but there was no fence and the trees were smaller. I couldn't see it at the time."

"Then that must be your mother," said Hannah, pointing at the little girl. "So what's the connection between her and Eric?"

She turned it over. "*Gee-up Mum. August 62*," she read from the back.

"These might tell us something," she said, picking up and peering into a faded folder. "It's certificates or something."

She pulled the top one out. David read the clear print out loud:

NATIONAL CYCLING PROFICIENCY
CERTIFICATE
awarded to
ERIC ROBINSON
20.5.64

"Eric Robinson?" breathed Hannah, her eyes visibly widening. "Eric is your mother's brother! Did you know she had a brother?"

"No, I didn't," said David quietly. "She never

talked about her family at all. I don't understand. Why is it all hidden away? What did he do?"

"That makes Eric your uncle."

"Uncle Eric," said David slowly, sounding the words.

"That happens sometimes," Hannah informed him. "It's all to do with your genes. Physical similarities skip a generation, or several even, and you end up looking like your Great-Great-Uncle Wilfred."

Or your Great-Aunt Jess, thought David.

"Look, there's even a baby shoe down here." She yanked out a tiny, flattened, red button-strap shoe.

"We're never going to sort this out before they get back," said David. "It'll take days to do it properly."

He dug his hand deeply under the loose piles and peered in.

"There are some school exercise books here, and some drawing pads."

He pulled them out. Hannah picked up one of the faded exercise books. "*Eric Robinson, 2S, History*."

She flicked the pages.

"Hey, listen, 'Tyrannosaurus Rex was the fiercest of the dinosaurs. His name means thunder lizard.' Some things never change," she said. "We did that in 2J."

But David was staring at a page in a drawing pad: a picture showing the earth and its planets. It was like seeing one of his own drawings. In fact, he had an almost identical one at home on his wall. The meticulous shading, the cross-hatching of colour, the highlighting could all have been done with his own hand.

He turned the pages slowly, staring at the painstaking images of astronauts, planets, moonscapes, craters and spaceships that coloured the pages.

"What is it?" said Hannah. "Have you found something?"

"I can't believe it," he said. "These drawings – they're just like the ones I do – they could be mine. I'll show you later."

As he flicked through another of the drawing pads, Eric ceased to be the mysterious intruder that he'd felt him to be yesterday. This Eric was someone he knew, identified with, liked. Someone he wanted to know better. He wanted to meet Eric. Why had Mum never given him the chance?

"There's something quite big further down," said Hannah, tugging hard. Finally, she extracted a large, flat rectangular package.

"Look, it's still got wrapping paper round it. It's faded but you can still see the moons and stars. Hold on, there's a label underneath – '*To Eric on your 11th birthday with love from Mum, Dad and Linda*'."

They looked at one another.

"He never opened it," said Hannah.

Chapter Twelve

"They've been gone an hour and ten minutes," said David. "We'd better put this lot back."

"It can't be – I was supposed to feed Blossom five minutes ago," said Hannah, shovelling everything back into the case.

"I'm holding on to this for a bit," David said, slipping one of the drawing pads down his tee-shirt. "I just hope I can put the key back before he notices."

They stood in Auntie Bird's hallway watching Blossom lapping furiously at her milk as the three kittens scrabbled blindly at one another, giving out tiny squeaks. Blossom stopped to look at them anxiously.

"You know what I'm thinking?" said Hannah suddenly.

"What?"

"You may not like it."

"Get on with it."

She took a deep breath.

"I think Eric's dead."

The thought had occurred to David too, but he had pushed it away. And he wasn't going to say it. While it remained unspoken, he could still hope. He could wonder what would Eric be like now. Would he still be drawing pictures of craters and moonscapes? Or would he be checking his engine oil, flicking the T.V. channel over from the funny bit in 'Red Dwarf' to catch the News on the other side, discussing the merits of matt versus silk finish for the kitchen walls, instructing his children, (did he have children?), in stage three of the washing-up? It was important to know.

David shrugged at Hannah's suggestion.

They went into the kitchen where Auntie Bird had left some coffee cake and squash for them.

"I wonder who took that photo of them in the garden?" said David.

"It could have been Aunt Jess," said Hannah, wiping crumbs off her mouth with the back of her hand. "You ought to ask her about it. If anyone knows anything, it's her."

There was the sound of a key turning in a lock.

"Coo-ee! Hannah! David! We're back."

David lay on his bed, his hands behind his head, staring at the ceiling, but not seeing it. He was seeing the empty blue room across the landing and the look of astonishment on Grandad's face when he'd waved, the way he nearly lost his balance and had to step back. He was seeing Grandad at the kitchen table, turning over the pages of his drawing book and silently sliding it back into place, without a word. He was seeing his expression on the day of the funeral when he'd stepped through the back door and Grandad had said, "I could pick him out in a crowd anywhere", even though he hadn't seen him for six years.

Eric was his uncle but he was also Grandad's son. And here he was, David, in Grandad's house, looking just like him, drawing pictures like him and Grandad hadn't said a word. Until the day before yesterday, he'd never heard of Eric. What was going on?

He sat up, walked to his door and crossed the landing. He stood for a few seconds with his hand on the door knob to the blue room, then slowly turned the handle and stepped in.

This must be where Eric had slept, drawn his pictures, built cranes from Meccano, laid on his bed, chuckling at Dennis the Menace and Gnasher. He looked around him. There were dark rectangles on the walls and flaking paint where pictures were once mounted, then pulled off.

In full sunlight, with the window shut, the room seemed to swell and hum with heat.

He undid the window catch and pushed it open, narrowing his eyes at the glint of the river below as a cool breeze slipped in. He stretched out on the seat.

How many times had Eric sat here, watching the same river flow past, he wondered? He remained there for some time, almost willing Eric to appear and explain it all. Quite suddenly he wanted to believe in ghosts. He wouldn't be scared: not of Eric.

And then he was hearing the words that had leaked through the closed door at home, when Dad had shouted to Mum, "I'm not going to let her ruin this family too!"

What had Nan Robinson done to ruin the family? Had she done something to Eric? Something unpredictable? That was the word Dad had used. Was this why everything had been shoved away in the shed, pushed under a bit of old carpet, hidden away in the dark: a terrible secret that no one would talk about?

When Hannah called after dinner, supposedly to work on the kite, it was with little enthusiasm that he made his way to the shed. It all seemed rather pointless. He had seen inside the suitcase and although he wanted to look again, he wanted more than that now. He wanted answers to his questions. He wanted to speak to people who knew Eric, to ask them what he was like. He wanted more than photos and certificates.

They had almost finished the kite and Hannah was painting the design. He sat on the work-bench playing with the vice, rattling the metal handle backwards and forwards in its socket.

He'd wanted an astronaut, but she'd wanted a whale and he couldn't be bothered to argue.

"For goodness sake, can't you leave it alone!" she snapped. "You're driving me nuts."

He shoved his hands into his pockets and started to kick the legs of the bench.

"I've been thinking," said Hannah as she put the final touches to the whale's tail.

David raised his eyebrows in feigned interest. In his opinion, she did too much thinking.

"About how we can check whether Eric died."

"Go on then."

"I'll tell you later," she said.

When the kite was finally finished, they strapped it onto Hannah's bike and set off in the direction of Badbury Rings. But unexpectedly, Hannah suddenly turned off into a narrow lane that David half-recognised. As they rode through a pointed arch-way, David realised they were in the cemetery where Nan Robinson had been buried. Hannah parked her bike.

"I thought we were going to Badbury Rings. What are you playing at?" he demanded, without dis-mounting.

Hannah continued securing her bike chain as if she hadn't heard. Then she stood up, put her hands on her hips and said, "I thought you wanted to know if Eric was dead or not!"

"Oh, so we go round searching every grave, every headstone for clues do we? This place is vast – it would take days. I know. I've been here before, re-member?"

"Look, if you're not interested in finding out, just say so. I've got plenty of other things I could be doing, you know," scowled Hannah.

"As long as it's not one of your stray theories about twins and criminal fathers," said David.

Hannah stared at him, then wordlessly returned to her bike, removed the padlock, jumped on and scooted towards the gate.

"Hey, wait!" David cried, moving forward quickly and blocking her exit.

She stopped and glared at him.

"O.K. I'm sorry," he muttered.

She folded her arms and stared upwards at a tree.

"I didn't mean it, honestly. I APOLOGISE."

She looked at him blankly.

"Look, I'm really, really sorry. I do want to know – and if you know how to find out, I shall be eternally grateful. O.K. now?"

She smiled triumphantly, parked her bike, and re-chained the padlock.

"It's quite simple when you know where to look," she announced.

"How come you know so much about it?" David asked in the politest tones he could manage.

"We had to do individual local history projects last term. I did Deaths, Graves, Tombs And Burials of Wimborne. I'm very well informed."

"Well, it's a change from ponies and ballet," said David, thinking of Kelly and Emma with whom he'd shared his table at school.

"I'm talking about local history," protested Hannah, "not stupid little hobbies. Mrs Baker said it was the most original project she'd ever seen. I got an A and they put it on display in the school library."

They were walking across an area of soft grass where flat sloping stones, like old-fashioned desk lids, were laid out in lined ranks.

"These are for the cremations," she informed him.

"They bury the ashes here. Did you know that one of the founding fathers of cremation lived in Wimborne? They called him Stoker Hanham.

"I love cemeteries," she proclaimed. "They tell you all sorts of things, but they make you want to know more."

She led the way past neat hedges and clipped trees that looked as if they had escaped from a Noddy-in-Toyland illustration.

Now they were walking past graves and headstones bubbling with yellow lichen, where illegible words mutely defied reading. Some were blackened, some crumbling. There were scrolls, angels, open books, imposing arches and looming crosses.

"Typically Victorian," Hannah informed him confidently.

They were approaching another tomb of heavy, dark, oppressive stone, surrounded by spiky, linked chains on great pillars. David wondered if the purpose was to keep passers-by out or its occupant firmly shut in.

"Look at this one," instructed Hannah. She pointed to a huge cross, draped with an anchor and chain.

IN LOVING MEMORY OF OUR DARLING
DAUGHTERS
HILDA, MAUDE AND FLORENCE
TAKEN SO TRAGICALLY
5TH DECEMBER 1892

"Doesn't it just make you want to know what

happened?" she demanded, flinging her arms dramatically outwards.

"I'm quite an expert on graves," she continued. "I'll show you the man with two left feet sometime," she promised, "and the man buried in the wall."

She saw the look on David's face.

"Really," she insisted. "They're not here though."

She waved to a man in the distance, pushing a wheelbarrow.

"That's Neville," she said. "I interviewed him for my project. It was a chapter called 'A Day in the Life of a Cemetery'. And then I interviewed an undertaker, and someone at the Crematorium. It's really interesting. You can read it sometime, but it's not for the squeamish."

"Where are we going exactly?" asked David, who had noticed they were taking a circuitous route.

"Over there," she indicated. "Where they do the recent burials."

"That's where Nan was buried, I think," said David.

"Exactly," said Hannah knowingly. "That might tell us what we want to know."

"I don't get it," said David.

Hannah had stopped to read the inscription beneath a huge winged angel. "Look, he was only three," she said. "Poor thing. Children died young in those days."

"One of the things I found out," she confided as they set off again, "is that when someone is buried, you have to buy a burial plot. That is, unless someone in your family has been buried there before and there's still room in the same plot for another coffin."

"What, they jam them in all together?" said David.

"Well, they sort of stack them, to save space. You can have three or four coffins to one plot. That's why you get several names on one headstone."

"What, they dig it up each time and add a new one?" said David, getting interested.

"They don't dig up the previous coffin – they just dig down to that level, ready for the next one. You know, in layers."

They had slowed down now and David's mind was working on the implications of what Hannah had just told him.

"So you see," Hannah continued, "if Eric did die, it's likely that he would be buried here, and that your nan would be buried in the same plot. I worked it all out last night, when I couldn't get to sleep."

"Hang on," said David, stopping. "It doesn't really help us does it? We can't go digging her up to find out."

"We don't have to," said Hannah with exasperation. "The headstone will tell us."

"What headstone?" said David. "She didn't have a headstone. I'd have noticed."

"That's because it gets sent away, so that they can engrave the new name on it. Then they put it back when it's finished. It's like a list. They just keep adding new names until it's full up, or the plot is full."

"So, if they're buried in the same plot, the headstone will have both names on," said David.

"Come in, number two," sighed Hannah.

"What are we waiting for, then?" he yelled. "Come on!" and off he ran.

"I'm sure it was round here somewhere," he called as Hannah caught him up, panting slightly.

He trotted along a row of headstones separated by neatly mowed lawn, scanning the inscriptions. He stopped when he reached the end. "I'm certain it was round here," he said, puzzled. "I remember, it was near someone called Henry – Henry Lewinson."

They walked back slowly together.

"There it is," said Hannah suddenly. "Henry Arthur Lewinson."

But the plot next to it had no headstone. They stared down at the anonymous grave.

"This must be it," said David. "Look you can still see the marks where they've replaced the turf. But where's the headstone?"

Hannah stood, arms folded, frowning in disappointment.

"We could ask Neville," she suggested brightly. "Come on – he might know."

She led the way towards a small steepled building in the centre of the cemetery, which reminded David of a church, but turned out to contain rollers, mowers, wheelbarrows and various gardening and digging implements.

"Hi, Neville!" she called to a man sitting on a large, bulging sack, drinking something from a cup.

"Oh, it's you again, is it?" he said. "You'll end up

haunting this place. Want a sandwich?" he said offering them a plastic box.

"No thanks," said Hannah. "This is David. His gran is buried here."

Neville nodded sympathetically. "As good a place as any," he commented as if he were recommending a hotel.

"She's over there," said Hannah pointing vaguely towards a wheelbarrow. David had an overwhelming urge to laugh.

"The thing is, we found the grave, but there's no headstone," she explained.

Neville chewed thoughtfully.

"When was she buried then?" he asked David after some while.

"About two weeks ago."

"Ah, well then. There's your answer," said Neville, nodding. "Mystery solved."

They stood there waiting for Neville to enlarge on this statement but he was now busy with pouring himself another drink from his flask. "Decaffeinated," he informed them, waggling his flask. "The other stuff makes me hyperactive."

"No," he continued taking another sandwich, "there wouldn't be a headstone, not after two weeks."

Hannah was getting impatient. David could tell by the way she was leaning on her hip and shuffling her feet and looking up at the ceiling.

"Why not, Neville?" she demanded.

"It's the ground, see – it has to settle. At least a

couple of months that is. And then there's your headstone itself, or your memorial plaque or your engraved urn, or whatever you've decided to commemorate your departed with, it's all got to be chosen and ordered, and made to specifications, hasn't it? These matters can't be rushed."

"Well, we think there might have been a headstone already," interrupted David, "from a previous burial."

"Still applies," said Neville. "Still has to go off to the mason's to be engraved."

"Where would it be now then?" asked Hannah.

"Now you're asking," said Neville, shaking out his lunch box. "All depends on which firm of undertakers or stonemasons your family used. That's if they've got that far," he said to David. "It's not a thing people should rush into. Those monuments are going to be around for a long time. Tell you what," he said, "come back in six months. Should all be in place by then."

"That's that then," sighed David as they made their way back to the bikes.

"I shall donate my body to medical research," declared Hannah.

Chapter Thirteen

They were turning out of the cemetery when Hannah braked suddenly. David only just managed to avoid crashing into her.

She had that look again. David could almost see a light bulb flashing above her head, with the words, IDEAS AND THEORIES stamped on it.

She looked at her watch.

"Mum's still at work," she announced as if she had just seen a vision in its dial. "She doesn't get home till half-past three on Fridays."

"Riveting," said David.

"It means," she said with emphasis, "that we can go back to my house and use the phone."

"Wonderful," mocked David. "I can ring up Grandad and say, 'Hello, Grandad. I'm at Hannah's and I'm using her phone'."

"Oh, you're *so* dense!" she cried between clenched teeth and looking skyward.

"I'm not!" protested David.

"Look – it means we can try ringing around some of the local stonemasons, or whatever they're called and make some polite enquiries."

"Polite enquiries?" said David.

"Yes," said Hannah. "You know, about the headstone we asked to be engraved."

A slow grin of understanding spread across David's face.

They sat at the bottom of the stairs with the *Yellow Pages* open before them.

"Try funerals first," said Hannah. "There it is – *Funeral Directors*."

They scanned the pages.

Didcott and Sons,
Funeral Services
memorials supplied
Roger Halesworth Ltd.
Funeral Director and Monumental Mason.

"There's quite a few," said David, turning the pages.

"Let's start with this one," said Hannah. "I'll do it if you like," and without waiting for an answer she dialled a number.

"Hello, yes, this is the daughter of Mr Robinson. My father ordered a headstone for his wife, Mrs Robinson – her full name? . . ." she gave David a panicked look.

"Estelle," David muttered.

". . . yes, Estelle Robinson," she continued. "It was about two weeks ago – can you tell me when it will be ready? Thank you."

She covered up the mouthpiece and whispered to David, "They're looking it up."

"Hello, yes?" she said returning to the phone. "Oh

dear, I must have made a mistake. Sorry to bother you."

She put down the phone and they both collapsed with laughter.

The next five attempts were just as unsuccessful.

"Try this one," suggested David. "Jackman and Styler."

"I wonder if you can help me . . ." said Hannah.

David sat at the bottom of the stairs as Hannah, much more convincing after several unproductive attempts, launched into her polite enquiry.

Suddenly, she turned to David and raised her eyebrows in surprise.

"You've just started work on it. Oh good. I wonder, could you just remind me of the entire inscription – I've mislaid my copy. Yes, I'll hold on."

"They've gone out to the workshop," she whispered.

She stood with pencil poised over the phone pad.

"Yes, I'm still here. Can you go slowly so that I can write it down?"

David stood up and watched as the pencil slowly printed out its message:

ERIC GORDON ROBINSON
DEEPLY BELOVED SON
OF GEORGE AND ESTELLE ROBINSON
AND BROTHER OF LINDA
BORN 6 AUGUST 1954 – DIED 5 AUGUST 1965
ALSO
HIS MOTHER ESTELLE MAY ROBINSON

BORN 15 APRIL 1926 – DIED 4 JULY 1991
AT PEACE AT LAST

"Thank you very much," said Hannah putting down the phone.

They stood silently reading the words to themselves. Then without looking up, David said,

"He died the day before his eleventh birthday. And what's more – he's got the same birthday as me."

He sat on the stair, holding the piece of paper in his hands. He was surprised by his overwhelming sense of disappointment. And something else too. He hadn't felt anything for Nan at all. But with Eric, he felt as if he'd lost someone he'd known all his life.

Hannah leaned against the wall, watching and waiting.

At last he said, "Well done, Hannah. At least I know."

David sat resting his chin on his knees, looking at Hannah try to launch the kite, but his thoughts were elsewhere. He was going over the events of the last few days concerning Eric and Grandad, trying to gather the pieces together, shuffling them around to make a complete picture.

Eric was dead: Mum's brother, Grandad's son, his uncle – was dead. Until this week, he'd never heard of Eric: never been aware of his existence. Had he not been idly poking about in Grandad's shed, he would have remained a secret. Why? Why? Why? He pulled up a handful of grass and watched as the wind snatched it from him.

"I'm getting the hang of this – it nearly took off then," shouted Hannah.

David looked up. "Try running down the hill with it," he called.

"Hey, look!" she yelled, and he saw the kite lift and tug and the string tauten as Hannah struggled to unwind the reel.

"Don't you want a go?" she shouted five minutes later. "It's great – flies like a bird."

He walked over and she passed the reel over.

"The wind's really strong," said Hannah. "Makes your arms ache after a bit."

"I expect Eric would have come out here," she said after a while. "It's really weird that no one in your family has ever mentioned him. I wonder how he died."

"I don't know," said David. "But there are those who do, and somehow, I'm going to find out."

"How?"

"I'm going to ask," he said, "starting with Auntie Bird."

The kittens were asleep when David and Hannah looked.

"Poor Blossom – the first rest she's had all day," said Auntie Bird, bending over them. "She's been licking and feeding non-stop. That grey one's the worst. Always hungry – pushes the others out of the way. You can tell who's going to be boss."

She straightened up. "And what have you two been doing with yourselves?" she asked as they went into the kitchen.

"Flying the kite," said Hannah who was reaching out for a cherry on a tray of buns.

Auntie Bird slapped her hand away. "You leave those alone, young lady! They're for the fête tomorrow – I hope you've got nothing planned. This will all need carrying across to the school field and I'm relying on you two."

She gestured to the boxes, tins, trays and packets of cakes, biscuits, flans and pies that she was pricing up with sticky labels.

"Here you are," she said, offering a couple of sad-looking buns. "Have one of these – Marjorie's cakes leave a lot to be desired – but don't you let on I said so."

"And wonders will never cease, David," she continued, picking up the kettle and starting to fill it at the tap. "I've managed to persuade your grandad to come along and help on the produce stall."

She turned away to set a tray of tea-cups and immediately Hannah started to roll her eyes and frown and mouth ERIC at him.

Everything seemed to slow down. He'd promised himself he would ask, but now it came to it, it was much more difficult than he'd imagined. But if he didn't ask now, it would be too late. He was leaving the day after tomorrow, and anyway, he was sure that if he didn't say something quickly, Hannah was going to suffer permanent injury from her facial distortions.

"Auntie Bird," he heard his voice say. "What happened to Eric?"

Auntie Bird stopped as if pause-framed and David counted the seconds until she said, "Eric who?"

"Eric Robinson," said David. "My uncle."

She turned round very slowly.

"How could you possibly know about Eric?" she asked.

"I found some photos in the shed."

Auntie Bird pulled a chair from under the table, and sat down heavily.

"Well, well. You do surprise me – in the shed, you say?"

"Yes," said David. "There's a suitcase full of stuff, games, books, photos, old school stuff – I haven't seen it all yet."

"He kept them then . . ." she said, but she wasn't really talking to David. "All this time, and he kept them – but I thought . . ."

She saw them watching her and added hurriedly, "but never mind what I thought. Tell me what you know, David."

"Well, I know he was Grandad's son and Mum's brother – and that I look like him – and I know that he died the day before his eleventh birthday."

Auntie Bird nodded. She looked quite shaken by the news.

"But what happened, Aunt Jess? How did he die? Why is it such a big secret?" begged Hannah.

Auntie Bird lifted her hands helplessly and let them drop again. She paused then said, "I made a promise. A long time ago, I made a promise. I sometimes wished that I never had. But I've kept to it and I won't break it."

David and Hannah stood in mute disappointment.

"But if you ask me," she said, looking at David, "it's time it all came out into the open. And there's only one person who can tell you, David, and that's your grandfather."

Chapter Fourteen

"When are you going to ask him then?" said Hannah as she sprawled across the seat in the shelter at the rec..

"As soon as I get the chance," said David. "I have to – I'm leaving on Sunday. Hey, I brought this to show you."

He drew out two drawing pads from his rucksack.

"Hold on," he said. "Close your eyes first."

He opened both pads at a certain page and spread them out on the seat between them.

"Right, look now."

"So?" she said, studying them both.

"One of these is mine, one is Eric's."

"Crumbs, it's truly creepy. They're so alike."

She picked them up and turned to the covers.

THE PROPERTY OF ERIC ROBINSON.
KEEP OUT

announced one. The other said:

MARTIAN TERRITORY
EARTHLINGS KEEP OUT

"Martian territory?" sneered Hannah.

"It's my nickname – Martian."

"Perhaps you're Eric's reincarnation," she suggested. "Cast your mind back to August 1965," she chanted, staring into his eyes and waving her fingers. "How did you die?"

"You really ought to meet Eva," said David, recoiling from her tentacling fingers. "You two would get on like a house on fire."

A toddler wobbled past them on a miniature bike with stabilisers. Beyond him, across the field, the windows of the houses in Redcott Road watched, just as they had once watched Eric on his tricycle.

"What do you think happened to him?" said Hannah, stretching herself out so that David was squeezed into the corner of the seat. It was clear from her manner that she had another theory.

"You really want to know?" he said.

"Oh, get on with it!" she demanded impatiently.

"I think my nan had something to do with it."

He watched her face. It was the dead body in the wardrobe expression again.

"Your nan? You don't think she killed him?"

"I didn't say that. But I think she had something to do with it. She was always very strange – and then Dad told me something, just before I came to stay with Grandad. He said she'd had a mental illness, that sometimes she did unpredictable things. That's why the family visits stopped."

He could almost hear the drive-belt whirring as Hannah processed the information.

She leant forward.

"Think hard," she said. "Can't you remember anything about her that would give you a clue?"

"All I can remember is that she didn't *do* anything. Just sort of sat there, glaring, and staring into space. I used to be quite frightened of her. I remember thinking she didn't like me. If she did have something to do with it, it would explain why no one ever talked about it.

"Anyway," he continued, "what about you? I bet you've got a theory."

"Not any more," said Hannah. "Yours is much more interesting."

Grandad wasn't in the garden when David got back. Or in the kitchen. He made his way upstairs.

"Is that you, David?" called Grandad.

He appeared at the bathroom door in vest and loose dangling braces with his razor in his hand and his face lathered.

"Have you got some clean clothes?" asked Grandad, returning to the mirror and ploughing a furrow with his razor across the foam.

"I've got a tee-shirt and shorts I haven't worn yet."

"Good," said Grandad, swirling his razor in the scummy water. "When I've finished you can have a wash and change. We are going out."

He splashed water onto his face, pulled the plug and patted his face with a towel as the water gurgled away.

"Only one more day," he said, "and you'll be on your way home. So tonight, I'm taking you, and Jess and Hannah to the pictures. But we'll have a bite to eat somewhere first, eh?"

He looked at David.

"Thanks, Grandad. Auntie Bird didn't mention it though, when we saw her."

"No, she wouldn't have," said Grandad. "I only thought of it ten minutes ago. She's taking us in her car. But it's my treat. Haven't been to the pictures for years."

As he came out of the bathroom David realised something was different. The door to the blue room was open, the window on its latch: Grandad had been in there.

As David searched the bottom of his bag for clean clothes, he became aware of some very confused feelings. One was relief that he could put off asking Grandad about Eric and one was frustration at still not knowing. He couldn't identify the others.

Chapter Fifteen

On Saturday morning there was a postcard next to David's cereal bowl. He glanced briefly at the boring picture of a windmill and turned it over. It had been forwarded by Mum, from home.

HAVING A GREAT TIME
SEE YA
MARK

He pulled his left ear twice.

All of them, including Grandad, reported for duty to Auntie Bird who issued orders regarding trestles, the setting up of, table tops, the fetching and covering of with tablecloths, cakes and goods the delivering of and various other tasks. They scurried to and fro in ant-like trails amongst other helpers and were astonished by how well-ordered everything was by the grand opening time.

There were so many cakes, that they needed two tables and still did not have enough space to set them all out. One minute it was all calm and peace and the next people were surging towards them and they were swept along in the rush of counting biscuits and rock buns, giving change, wrapping cakes, bagging coconut pyramids and turning their brains into cash registers as hands held out cakes and money and voices demanded to know if it was fresh cream or whether this contained animal fat or eggs or tartrazine.

An hour and twenty minutes later the white paper tablecloths were torn and covered with crumbs and blobs of butter cream and all that remained was a lurid green sponge cake and a few of Marjorie's buns. Auntie Bird sent them off to check on Blossom and her kittens and to give them time to explore the rest of the fête.

"This is my favourite one," said Hannah, holding the grey kitten to her shoulder.

"The bossy one," observed David. "I like this one – he looks like Korky in *The Dandy*."

The kittens miaowed soundlessly and clawed the air as they held them up.

They returned to the fête. Hannah won a false nose and moustache in the lucky dip, which David said was an improvement, so she embarrassed him for the rest of the afternoon by wearing it.

By now the raffles had been called, the prizes given and the band was packing away its instruments. They sat on the grass, licking their ice creams, and watching a small boy lying spreadeagled on his back, silently refusing to respond to his mother's pleas to get into his pushchair.

"When do you go back?" asked Hannah.

"Tomorrow morning – I'm catching the coach from Poole."

"What about Eric, then?"

"I shall have to ask Grandad tonight," said David, a great deal more confidently than he felt.

They drove back home in Auntie Bird's car, the boot rattling with unclaimed cake tins and boxes.

"Ninety pounds eighty-three pence," boasted Auntie Bird. "We always do well on cakes."

They dropped Hannah home on the way. It was only as they drove off that David realised he hadn't said goodbye. And he was cross with himself at the awareness that it mattered to him more than he thought it should.

"Well, David, your last evening here," said Grandad, when they got home. "You can choose what we have for tea."

"Onion soup," said David.

And Grandad actually smiled.

The phone in the hall rang and Grandad hurried to answer it. It was Mum.

"No – we'll take the bus into Poole. Jess has offered to take us in, but she's done enough already."

"No – no trouble at all. In fact, he's been quite a help."

David used his knuckles to polish an imaginary medal on his chest, as he listened from the kitchen.

"David – your mum," called Grandad. "She wants a quick word."

"Just checking everything's all right for tomorrow,

David," said Mum. "We'll meet you at Victoria. We'll get there in good time in case you're early. Then we'll find somewhere for lunch. Would you like that?"

"Mum . . ." said David.

There was silence on the line while he tried to choose the right words.

"Are you still there, David?" said Mum.

"Mum – can I stay on a bit longer – you know – with Grandad?"

There was another silence. He could hear Mum's voice fade and say, "He wants to stay on . . ."

Her voice grew loud again.

"David? If that's what you want, it's fine with us. I can easily change your ticket. Is Grandad happy about you staying?"

"I dunno – I haven't asked him yet."

"What?"

"Well – I only just thought of it. You see, well – it's O.K. here."

For a moment the line was silent again. Then Mum spoke.

"Look, let me have another word with Grandad." He could hear an animated conversation going on in the background between Mum and Dad.

But Grandad had been listening. He appeared at the kitchen doorway holding an onion. He looked directly at David as he took the phone.

"No problem at all," Grandad said. "It'll be a pleasure. You leave him with me. We get on just fine."

*

David said it. Just as Grandad started to slice the onions. And once he'd started, he couldn't stop.

"Grandad – I know about Eric – and I know he's dead – that he died the day before his birthday – which is the same as mine – but I don't know why because no one's ever talked about him – Mum or Dad or you – and I've asked Auntie Bird but she won't say – she says she made a promise – and she says – she says that I should ask you."

He looked up from the table at which he had been staring as the words had poured out of him. He saw Grandad standing there with his back to him, grasping the knife in one hand and the edge of the worktop with the other, and his knuckles white.

"I know he looked like me – I've seen photos – and he drew pictures like me – I've seen them all in the case in the shed – but I don't know how he died – or why I've never been told about him. I don't understand. Please, Grandad, please – what happened to Eric?"

He saw Grandad open his mouth as if to speak but the only sound was the tick of the old plate clock. He watched, waiting, willing Grandad to tell him.

Grandad made a small sound, like a dry cough, and David had to strain to hear the words.

"He drowned . . ." Grandad croaked. "He drowned. Eric drowned – at the bottom of the garden."

He dropped the knife and David watched the old man's face fight against the tears that started to stream down his face. He covered his face with a hand as he scrabbled in his pocket for a hanky, but as he brought it up, his hand caught the edge of the chopping board, and knife, board and onions crashed to the floor.

David had sat there, paralysed into helplessness by the sight of Grandad's tears, but now he could do something. He leapt up, led Grandad to a chair and started to pick up the mess from the floor, wondering if he should go and fetch Auntie Bird.

Grandad sat at the table, his head in his hands. David stood watching, overwhelmed with remorse at what he had done to Grandad. Then, quite suddenly Grandad reached out a hand and took hold of David's, clenching it so tightly that he could feel Grandad's nails digging into his palm. And then he spoke.

"Do something for me, David. Pop round to Jess's – I need to be on my own for a bit."

David stood up.

"Are you sure, Grandad – are you sure you'll be all right? I'm sorry – I didn't mean . . ."

Grandad wiped his face and looked at him.

"No, you're right. You should be told – just give me time."

As David reached the back door, he said, "Tell Jess she's kept her promise for long enough."

David sat in one of Auntie Bird's soft chairs.

"Do you think I should go back?" he asked.

"No, leave him be for a while. He needs to cry and he's not the sort of man who'd want to be watched, David. The problem is, he never had the chance to grieve properly when Eric died: he's held it back for years."

"I still don't understand why it's been kept a secret," said David. "Was it something to do with Nan?"

"Yes – it was, in a way, but it's a long story," sighed Auntie Bird. "Look, I'll go and make a cup of tea and then I'll tell you all about it. Would you like a slice of cake?"

But David wasn't hungry.

Chapter Sixteen

David couldn't believe that making a pot of tea could take so long. He thought how useful it would be if people had fast forward buttons so that you could speed them up.

At last Auntie Bird bustled in with a tray, and then he had to wait while she set out the cups and saucers and milk jug and sugar bowl and pour the teas.

"What was he like, Auntie Bird?" he asked, unable to contain himself any longer.

She looked up at him.

"Oh, so much like you, David – especially to look at. It's quite true, you could be his double. That's what made it all so difficult. It might have been easier if you didn't."

David frowned in puzzlement.

"I'll explain later," she said. "I'll begin with the accident, though heaven knows, there's hardly a day passes that I don't think of it."

She stirred her tea slowly.

"It was during the summer holiday – 1965. My husband Frank was alive then – and Eric was bosom buddies with our son John. They'd started together in the infants and what with living next door to one another, well, they were hardly ever out of each other's company – they practically lived in each other's houses."

She put down her cup and stared at her lap.

"Well, that particular morning – it was a beautiful day I remember – they'd planned to put up the tent in Eric's garden – they were going to camp out for a few nights – you know the sort of thing."

David nodded.

"But Frank, my husband, wanted John to go with him to the garden centre to help him load some compost. John moaned a bit – he didn't want to keep Eric waiting – but I insisted – and many's the time I've wondered if things would have been different if I hadn't – I insisted he helped his dad, so off they went."

She stopped and looked at David.

"Now what actually happened I didn't see, David, but the next thing I know is little Linda screaming and shouting and calling for me, so I rush round and there's your Grandad kneeling on the grass, and Eric stretched out all wet, and your Grandad shouting 'He's not breathing! He's not breathing!'"

She took a tissue from her pocket and blew her nose.

"You'll have to excuse me, David. I still can't think about it without getting upset."

David swallowed hard. A tear slowly trickled down her cheek and it was all he could do to hold back his own.

"Well, I knew what to do, I'd done a first-aid course and I managed to get him breathing. We thought everything would be all right then. But it was no use –

he'd been in the water too long. He died the following morning."

She shook her head helplessly and dabbed her eyes.

"It was just as well, I think. The doctor said he'd suffered severe brain-damage. He wouldn't have been the Eric we knew."

She looked up at the ceiling and blinked rapidly.

"But how did it happen?" asked David.

"Well, according to Linda, he was standing up in the boat – they used to have a little wooden rowing boat – he and John used to spend hours playing in it – he was standing up, when he just fell in. Linda didn't worry – she thought he was larking about, and he'd done it before, so she expected him to pop up again. But he didn't. By the time she'd realised something was wrong, he must have been in the water for a couple of minutes, then she had to rush off and find your grandad. He waded in and dragged him out and sent Linda to fetch me – but it was too late."

"Couldn't he swim?"

"Oh, yes. And John – they were both good swimmers. We wouldn't have let them use the boat otherwise. And the water wasn't deep – not more than hip-high. We don't know what happened exactly. They found a bruise on his head, but they couldn't be certain what happened."

She pressed her fingers against her eyes as if trying to blot it out.

"The strange thing is, even after all these years, I can still see every detail – Eric's red-striped tee-shirt, his bare foot where one of his plimsolls had come off when your grandad dragged him out, even the little tortoise-shell slide Linda was wearing in her hair . . ."

She picked up her cup of tea, which was now cold.

"The awful part –" she continued, staring at her tea, '– and I don't know how I did it – was waiting there to tell your nan about it. By then your grandad and Linda had gone off with Eric in the ambulance to the hospital. So I stayed round there. Estelle had gone shopping for Eric's birthday party. But John was the first to arrive. He came running round, shouting for Eric that he was back and I had to tell him about it. I don't think he took it in – he wanted to rush off to the hospital and ask Eric if he'd be all right for camping the next night."

She put down her tea, untouched.

"And then Estelle got back. When I told her she just went to pieces – started to run down the garden, shouting Eric's name. We had to drag her out of the water. She kept pushing us away, telling us we were lying . . ."

They sat there in the darkening silence.

"Well, we called the doctor and he gave her something to calm her down and later, Frank drove her out to the hospital. But it was no good – Eric never re-gained consciousness and he died early the next day."

They had forgotten the tea. David sat, huddled in his chair, visualising it all.

At last he said, "But why couldn't Mum have told me all this? I could have handled it. It was an accident – and years ago."

"Oh, David," breathed out Auntie Bird. "If only it were that simple."

She pushed herself out of her chair and walked over to the sliding glass doors, looking down to where the river glimmered like a silky ribbon in the distance.

Without turning, she said, "John, my son – he's an engineer in New Zealand now. Eric would be coming up to thirty-seven now. I often wonder what he would have become. He was such a bright boy."

"That's why he didn't open his birthday presents," said David. "We saw them, Hannah and me, in the suitcase."

"No," said Auntie Bird, turning back. "He would have been eleven the next day. There was going to be a party – Estelle had made the cake. It was going to be a surprise. She'd copied one of his drawings of the planets onto the icing – coloured it all in."

She began to tidy the cups onto the tray.

"Why did it make it worse, me looking like him?" asked David.

"I told you, it's a long story," said Auntie Bird, "and I think you've had enough for one night. Let's leave the rest, David, till later."

"Please, Auntie Bird," said David. "Please. I have to know."

She spread her hands in defeat and sat back in her chair.

"Well – I suppose that was just the start of it. Obviously we were all very shocked and upset at Eric's death. I remember, John cried for nights on end. But

Estelle just never got over it – she couldn't cope. She'd idolised Eric. Poor Linda not only lost her brother in the accident, she lost her mother too. To make it worse, she blamed Linda, then your grandad – said they'd allowed it to happen. The doctor had to put her on sedatives and she just took to her room. Wouldn't come out, wouldn't talk – not to your grandad or to Linda, hardly ate – wouldn't even go to the funeral. It was very hard on your grandad – he had to do everything and keep his job going. And Linda – she was only nine at the time – Linda had to grow up overnight. He was so busy with keeping everything ticking over and looking after your nan, he didn't have much time for her. It wasn't his fault – he did his best."

She sat, staring into the distance.

"The doctors said she'd probably get over it eventually," she continued, "but it didn't happen. Then one day, your grandad came home from work to find Estelle throwing Eric's things out of the window into the garden. She had torn the pictures off the walls, photos from albums – everything that reminded her of Eric – told him to burn it all, even the furniture. He tried to stop her, but she became hysterical – it was awful. We could hear her screaming from here. In the end, in an effort to placate her, that's what your grandad did. Built a big bonfire and set it alight."

She turned to David.

"That suitcase you found, he must have saved those from the fire. Poor man, couldn't bear to lose everything."

"And then," she continued, gesturing helplessly, "she just got worse and worse. Became aggressive if anyone mentioned Eric's name. Not only was she pretending that he hadn't died, but that he hadn't lived. Finally, your grandad made us all promise, including Linda, that we'd never mention Eric again. He hoped in time she'd recover. But in the end, she became so ill she had to go into hospital. She was there for a long time. Eventually they allowed her home, just weekends at first. But she was never the same again. She was like a stranger. She wouldn't, couldn't do anything. She moved into that downstairs room, and just shut out the world. Would sit for hours on end, just staring into space, or at the television, with the curtains drawn. It must have been terrible for your grandad. She'd been such a lovely person, full of fun – loved organising games and parties and outings. John adored her. But she just withdrew into her own world – surrounded herself with photos from her younger days as if she was still seventeen, as if she'd never married, never had children."

"Couldn't they make her better?" David asked.

"Oh, I'm sure they tried. But I don't think she wanted to get better. She wanted to escape. Your grandad managed to look after her and keep his job – with me helping out when I could, but it was hard work. It was Linda who suffered most, poor child. She could never take friends home. She even ran away once."

"Mum? Mum ran away?"

David couldn't believe it.

"Oh, yes," nodded Auntie Bird. "But I'm losing my thread. You'll have to ask your mum about that one."

"But other parents lose children, don't they? Children die, but they get over it," said David.

"No, David," she said shaking her head firmly. "No one gets over a thing like that, but they learn to come to terms with it. But not everyone is the same. Some can cope. Others can't. Estelle never got over Eric's death."

"I used to hear Mum and Dad row about it," said David, "when she came back from visiting. Dad used to say he wasn't going to let Nan ruin our family too."

Auntie Bird gave an understanding nod.

"It's been hard for your mum – and your dad. When she had you she wanted so much for it to be a normal family – didn't want your grandad to miss out on his new grandson, tried so hard to keep the family together."

"But she could have told me about Eric, couldn't she?"

Auntie Bird shook her head.

"She never talked about Eric – not even to me. Kept it all bottled up. And when you shut out something like that, it becomes a habit. You can't just open up and start talking about it – it's too painful, like opening a wound. She told your dad about it, but would never discuss it. And there was always the danger that you might just say something in front of your nan. The only time your mum gave in to her feelings was when she named you after him. It seemed like a minor miracle when you were born on Eric's birthday – you weren't due for another three weeks, and the fact that you resembled him so much. But she came to regret that later."

"Why?"

Auntie Bird studied him thoughtfully for a few seconds.

"Well, I suppose there's no harm in telling you now."

She leant forward.

"It was the last time your grandparents visited you in Bromley. You must have been about five. I'd gone to stay with my sister in Beckenham for Christmas and your mum had invited us both over for Boxing Day. She was expecting Lizzie – she was due in just a few weeks, so we were all giving a hand – clearing the table, washing up, that sort of thing – not Estelle of course. She was in her own little world. Anyway, we were all in the kitchen – we'd left you sitting at the table, drawing pictures with your new felt tips when there was a terrible crash and Estelle shouting.

"Well, we dropped everything and dashed in to find you lying on the floor and her standing over you calling you – calling you names."

"She called me a devil!" shouted David. "I remember – she called me a devil – an evil devil!"

Auntie Bird's jaw dropped and she clasped her hand over her mouth.

"Oh, David – I didn't want to bring that up – I'd

thought you'd forgotten – I shouldn't have reminded you."

"I don't remember it all," said David, "only the words. They came to me the other day when I was carrying that box of shoes and the slippers fell out. Why did she call me a devil, Auntie Bird?"

"Well, we tried to work it out afterwards. It appears that you'd drawn a picture and underneath you'd written DAVID ERIC MARSH. She'd torn it into pieces and later we tried to patch it together. We guessed you'd taken it over to show her. It must have triggered something in her memory – the name Eric, and the fact that you looked so much like him. We don't know what happened exactly. We think she must have pushed you away and that you fell against the table – you had a big gash on your head . . ."

David put his hand up to the scar above his eyebrow and Auntie Bird nodded.

". . . you were just lying there, blood pouring down your face and Estelle ranting on . . ."

She waved her hand as if trying to push away the memory.

"It was chaos – your grandad trying to calm her down, your mum in a terrible state kneeling over you, your dad trying to call an ambulance – in the end you had to spend a couple of days in hospital with concussion. It wasn't exactly the merriest of Christmas's.

"Later, your grandad discovered she hadn't been taking the pills he'd been giving her – she'd hidden them inside the pillow case. That's why she went out of control. But after that, your grandad wouldn't take any more risks. He stopped the visits except for your mum. You can't imagine what a painful decision that was for him, David. He'd grown so fond of you – and he's never seen Lizzie, ever. Only photos. Your mum tried lots of times to get him to let her go into a home, but he wouldn't hear of it. The last few years have been terrible for him, David, I can tell you. She didn't know who he was and he had to do everything for her. But he never complained. Just carried on looking after her."

Suddenly she smiled. "It must be quite a change for him having you here – and the best thing that could have happened if you want my opinion."

She stood up and picked up the tea tray.

"Do you know, that's just the same expression that Eric had. He used to stick his tongue to the corner of his mouth just like that. You could be Eric himself sitting there."

The room was dark now. She carried the tray out and as she left, David saw a shadow pass the glass doors and then heard Grandad's voice in the kitchen. But David was in no hurry. He had so much to think about. He could see Eric standing up in the boat, then topple and fall. And Mum sitting on the grass, not noticing, and then he was shouting at her, "Mum! Look, Mum! Can't you see – Eric's drowning! He's drowning!"

But she couldn't hear him. He was shouting and shouting – and then he could hear Eric calling to him, "David! Help me! Help me, David!"

He tried to leap up and run towards the river but

something held him back, something heavy on his shoulder.

"David! David!"

He opened his eyes. Auntie Bird was bending over him, gently shaking him.

"Bedtime for you, I think," she said.

As they made their way along the path Grandad put his arm around David. On the kitchen table was the open suitcase, some of its contents spilling out onto the table.

"We'll go through it tomorrow, eh David? Together."

Chapter Seventeen

After they had cleared away the breakfast things, Grandad lifted the suitcase back onto the table and David fetched the photo of Eric and the drawing books from his room.

"I borrowed these," he apologised. "And there's more at Hannah's – we took them there to get a proper look. I'll get them back later though."

Grandad stared at the photo.

"This must have been one of the last I took of him," he said.

"I thought it was me at first," explained David, "then I realised it couldn't be," and he went on to tell Grandad the whole story, but left out some of Hannah's more imaginative theories.

"And Auntie Bird told you the rest?" asked Grandad.

David nodded.

Slowly, Grandad started to turn the pages of the drawing book.

"Who would have believed you could be so alike?" he said, shaking his head.

They started to sift through the suitcase, Grandad sorting everything into piles as they did so. There were many more photos: some of the whole family, some of

Eric and Mum, some with a boy who Grandad pointed out as John Bird, photos of birthdays and Christmas and holidays and outings: the one thing they all had in common was Eric.

And as David studied them, he realised that Mum's past was here too, buried in this case. Her childhood had been lost, along with Eric's. Here she was on the swings at the rec. with Eric pushing her, here they both were, opening parcels before a Christmas tree, shiny-eyed with excitement, here was a birthday party, with Mum blowing out her six candles and Eric looking on. All her birthdays were here, doomed by Eric's image in the photos to be confiscated and abandoned.

Here too, were Nan and Grandad, fixed in time by the click of a camera, squinting into the sun on a beach, in the garden, smiling, smiling, smiling . . .

There were pictures of Eric and John: in Davy Crockett hats, in the boat, in cub uniforms, school trips . . .

How could anyone have guessed that all of this could have ended so suddenly at the bottom of the garden, or that this lively, laughing woman doing cartwheels on the beach or cutting a birthday cake could have shut herself away from the world in that drab room?

Each layer of the suitcase peeled back another layer of Eric's life: layers of other lives too: Mum's, Grand-ad's and Nan's. Like onions, thought David. Though these layers weren't in the right order: they were jumbled and overlapping and he had to re-arrange them in his head, sort them into the correct order. Each layer was important: it helped form the finished shape of the person.

"Does Mum know about all this?" asked David.

Grandad shook his head.

"I think it's time we told her, don't you?" said Grandad.

David dialled the number as Grandad stood behind him.

"Mum?"

"David? What a surprise!"

"Mum – I know all about Eric."

There was silence.

"Mum? I know. About how he died – everything."

Still there was no sound from the other end. He looked up helplessly to Grandad, who reached over and took the phone.

"Linda? Linda – it's all right. Please, Linda – don't – I think it's time we talked . . ."

David returned to the kitchen and shut the door. He could hear the low mumble of Grandad's voice, and after a long while, the receiver being replaced. Then there was the slow tread of Grandad's feet on the stairs. It was some time before he returned.

David had been right when he'd said that it would take days to go through the suitcase properly. By Sunday evening a large part of the contents had still not been touched, as Grandad took out each article, each picture and told its story. Eric had come alive, at least in

David's imagination, Mum, too and Nan Robinson. When Grandad mentioned her name now, the image of that grim, vacant face was fading into the young, smiling face from these photos.

You can't tell, thought David, just by looking, what people are really like. You have to peel back the layers.

They had now reached a large scrapbook. As Grandad lifted it and turned it over, David saw that it bore the title, written in faded felt-tips

SPACE EXPLORATION

"Wow," said David.

They turned the pages together, slowly.

"'The Space Age began,'" he read "'in 1957 when the Russians sent up Sputnik 1. I was only three then, so . . .'"

There were newspaper cuttings, photos, drawings and pictures from magazines, all carefully stuck in, though now some were loose: Major Yuri Gagarin looking out from his space helmet, or stepping from the doorway of a plane, or waving to the crowds who cheered the first man in space.

'John Glenn – First American to Orbit Earth' announced another caption further on.

Since then, man had walked on the moon, manned space-shuttles in countless orbits around the earth and launched space probes that sent back pictures of Mercury and Venus, Mars and Saturn and Jupiter. Eric had missed it all.

"He was mad about space," said Grandad. "Used to beg for everyone's old newspaper – you ask Auntie

Bird. You had to watch him though – he'd cut them up before you had a chance to read them. Could tell you anything – could store all the facts in his head."

As they reached the last few pages, a pile of loose cuttings fluttered. He read out loud from one of them.

"'Yesterday, Major Edward White became the first American to walk in space.'"

He looked at the date at the top of the page: 4th June 1965. Eric had never got round to sticking it in.

Chapter Eighteen

On Monday morning David called at Hannah's house. A tall slim woman with short, dark hair opened the door.

"Oh, so *you're* David," she beamed, as if several imposters had previously called under the pseudonyms of David Marsh.

"Do come in! How nice to meet you at last. Hannah, darling! Your friend David is here!"

David stepped in. Hannah's mum stared down at his feet, smiling. David wiped his trainers on the doormat for several minutes. Still she stared down. He levered them off at the heels. Satisfied, she disappeared into the kitchen, giving Hannah another shout as she went. Hannah's probably right, thought David: she is adopted.

Hannah appeared at the top of the stairs in her pyjamas.

"I heard you were still here. I hoped I'd got rid of you," she lied.

"Ditto," lied David. "Anyway, I haven't come to see you. I want the photos back to give to Grandad. I know it all now."

"Well, you're not having them. Not till you've told me EVERYTHING."

*

As they made their way slowly back to Grandad's, David told Hannah the whole story. Watching Hannah's face as he did so was not unlike reading a comic: every expression from shock to relief, from horror to tragedy passed across her face. He still hadn't finished when they reached Byron Road, so they detoured down the path to the river and sat on the bank.

"That's why he had the binoculars on the beach," interrupted Hannah, remembering. "He must have had the screaming hab-dabs every time you went near water. Especially with your birthday coming up – you know, history repeating itself and all that."

"You're dead morbid," decided David.

"I know," admitted Hannah proudly.

"Which reminds me," said David, "where's this man with two left feet?"

"What a let-down," announced David.

They were standing in the Minster, before the tomb of Sir Edmund Uvedale. The statue of a knight in full armour, reclining on one elbow, resting his head on his hand, was stretched before them. He clasped an armoured glove in the other hand, while gazing dreamily into the distance, as if out for a walk, on a sunny day, (in full armour), he had casually decided to lie down and watch the ducks. But there was definitely something wrong: he had two left feet.

"No wonder he's lying down," frowned David. "He'd have trouble walking."

"He'd have trouble standing up," observed Hannah, "with that lot on."

"Perhaps it's a faithful copy," suggested David. "Perhaps he was born with two left feet."

"No such luck," said Hannah, wandering off. 'The bloke who restored it mucked it up – in eighteen hundred and something.

"Here's the man-in-the-wall I told you about," she called.

David joined her and stared down at the large, heavy coffin set into the wall beneath a low arch. A plaque announced the name ANTHONY ETTRICK.

"He predicted his own death in 1693," informed Hannah, "and ordered his coffin to be made ready with the date engraved on the side. But he lived for another ten years, so they tried to alter the date, see."

She pointed to where the six had been altered, without much success, to a seven, and the nine to a nought.

"He also vowed that he would not be buried inside the minster, or outside, above the ground or below it, so they shoved him in the wall.

"Mad, if you ask me," she commented as they headed towards the door.

As they came out into the sunlight, the Quarter Jack chimed.

. . . and so will clang when I'm gone, thought David.

Grandad was coming out of the front room when David got back. When he looked later, there were several of Eric's school photos standing on the sideboard, along with a family photo, where Nan and Grandad, Eric and Linda stood, hand in hand before a lion guarding Nelson's Column.

He wandered across into Nan's room and stood staring at its bleak interior. Yet there was something different about it: had the room changed or had he? He couldn't decide. He picked up one of the framed photos from the chest: the one of Nan as a young girl, her arm around a boy.

"Who's this?" he asked Grandad who was preparing tea in the kitchen.

Grandad peered over his shoulder.

"Your nan's brother, Gordon."

"Wasn't that Eric's middle name?" asked David.

"Is there anything you don't know?" joked Grandad.

"Where is he now?"

"He was killed," said Grandad, putting down the teapot, "along with the rest of the family – a doodlebug in 1945. Your nan missed it – she was staying with a friend that night."

David stared at Nan and Gordon. Another layer, he thought. How different it would have been at Nan's funeral, if he'd known all of this.

"Grandad," he said as he sat down at the table, "can I move into Eric's room?"

Grandad looked up. "We'll move you in after tea," he said. "As soon as we've done the washing up."

*

"When do their eyes open?" asked Hannah as she bent over the kittens. Blossom had gone for a walk and the grey kitten was complaining loudly.

"Well, according to the book, twelve days or so," said Auntie Bird.

"That's very good, David," she continued, bending down over David and his drawing of two sleeping kittens. "All that with just a few strokes of a pencil."

"So – it's all set for next Tuesday then, is it?" she asked Grandad, who was sitting in her kitchen with a cup of tea.

"Mmmm," nodded Grandad. "They're all driving down on the morning of David's birthday, then David will go back home with them in the evening. Linda's bringing all his presents – and of course you're both invited. Phil says they should arrive about twelve."

David felt unexpectedly nervous waiting for the arrival of Mum and Dad and Lizzie. He felt at a distance from them: like strangers. It was only two weeks since he'd sat on the coach, dreading the days ahead of him, willing the time to pass, yet it seemed a lifetime away.

At precisely twelve o'clock he saw the car turn into the road. He should have known Dad would be precisely on time: he was the sort of man who would deliberately slow down to match his expected time of arrival.

He stood watching them get out of the car, Mum telling Dad to take care with the large tin, as it had the cake in it. Then suddenly she ran up, squeezed him hard, kissed him and said "Happy birthday, David," and he thought she was never going to let go. And then she was running over to Grandad and they stood there clasping one another, and when she stopped, her face was wet, and she was repeating it again with Auntie Bird, and she was dabbing her eyes too. David watched at a self-conscious distance, till he caught sight of Hannah crossing her eyes and pretending to throw-up and he laughed.

"Come on you two!" called Dad. "Lizzie and I can't carry it all – make yourselves useful."

"Come here, Lizzie," called Mum. "Come and meet Grandad."

And Lizzie advanced shyly, carrying a bottle of lemonade and Grandad was bending down, admiring her butterfly earrings.

Much to David's surprise, Hannah took Lizzie down the garden to see if there were any ducks: she had announced on a previous occasion that she did not like children and did not intend to get married, ever.

Grandad and Dad sat on the garden chairs and David caught fragments of conversation about hosepipe bans and holiday traffic, while Mum and Auntie Bird busied themselves in the kitchen. He knew he had to do something. He walked up to Mum and pulled her arm.

"Careful, David – you nearly knocked the plate out of my hand."

"Please, Mum. I want to show you something."

He looked to Auntie Bird, who put down her tray

and looked at Mum. Mum put down her plate and with a puzzled glance at Auntie Bird, followed him into the hall. He led her upstairs: to Eric's room. As he pushed the door open, her hands flew up to her face.

"I put them up," he said. "Some are Eric's, some are mine. I bet even you can't tell the difference."

She wandered slowly around, staring at the pictures on the wall of planets and spaceships. Then she walked over to the window, bending down to see the river.

"I used to come in here," she said quietly. "No one knew – sat here for hours. I used to wish for his ghost to visit. A ghost would have been better than nothing. I wouldn't have been frightened. Can you believe that?" she said, turning to David.

"Yes," he said. Then, "There's something else you should see."

She followed him downstairs to the front room, to the sideboard with its recently placed photos and the suitcase that had been moved from the kitchen to the sofa.

She flopped down next to it, reached out a hand and hesitated, as if by touching them, they would crumble, like burnt paper.

He rushed forward. "Look – there's loads with you in them – here's your sixth birthday party – and look, in fancy dress – and with Auntie Bird."

She shook her head, unbelieving.

Auntie Bird appeared in the doorway and beckoned him out. "We won't eat yet," she said to Mum. "How about a cup of tea though?" But Mum didn't hear.

*

"I couldn't eat another crumb," said Auntie Bird, licking the trifle spoon.

"Anyone for birthday cake?" called Mum. They all groaned: except Hannah. "Yes, please," she said.

Mum lit the candles, David blew them out, they all sang Happy Birthday and Dad took a photo. Then Dad went out to the car and reappeared with some parcels.

He had a drawing pencil and rubber from Lizzie, "from my own money," she insisted, a parcel of drawing pads from Auntie Bird, and a heavy long parcel from Mum and Dad.

"Fantastic, great!" he yelled when he'd unwrapped it. "A tent!"

"One more from us," said Dad taking something from his pocket.

David tore off the paper.

"A tin-opener?"

They all laughed.

"Oh, I almost forgot to tell you," said Mum. "Mark phoned this morning – they got back last night. He said to call him when you get back."

Grandad went inside and came out again. David instantly recognised what he was carrying: he could tell by the faded wrappings of moons and stars.

"I think he'd have liked you to have these," said Grandad.

David could feel everyone watching. This day, twenty-six years ago, Eric should have been doing this.

And he knew that Eric was here now: if not in the flesh, certainly in everyone's thoughts. He hesitated for a few seconds. It was silent, as if everything had stopped. He slowly tore back a strip of paper. The glimpse of shiny metal told him immediately what was inside. He tore off the remaining paper and lifted the lid of the large rectangular tin. Crayons: a complete set. Every shade of red and blue and green and yellow – the best quality too. He ran his finger along them, like a piano player.

"Thanks, Grandad," he smiled. "I've always wanted a set like this."

Grandad gave a stiff smile and handed him the next parcel. "A bit out-of-date now," he said.

"No," said David as he pulled off the paper to reveal *The Encyclopedia of Space Exploration.* "It's great."

He turned the cover.

To Eric with much love from Mum and Dad, August 6th 1965.

"Thanks."

No one said anything. The hot silence seemed to separate them.

Then Hannah said brightly, "I can't give you my present yet – not till your grandad has given you something else."

"Ah!" said Grandad, tapping his head as if just remembering. He took a key from his pocket and held it out: the key to the shed.

"This one's from Jess and me."

"Go on," he urged, seeing David's puzzled face. "You know where to look."

They watched David trot down to the shed and emerge a few seconds later, looking just as puzzled, holding a large basket. As he made his way back, Hannah held out her own parcel.

"This is to go with it," she instructed.

From the wrapping David withdrew a sturdy plastic dish.

They laughed at his confused expression.

"For your kitten," nudged Auntie Bird. "Your mum and dad have agreed that you can choose one of the kittens, though I think I know which one it's going to be."

"They're a bit young yet," added Grandad. "How about if me and Jess deliver him to you – in about six weeks or so?"

"The black and white one," grinned David. "I want the black and white one. And I'm going to call him Eric."

Chapter Nineteen

Dad had planned to leave by six, but the sky was growing dusky and the sun was sinking fast.

David and Hannah sat on the steps at the top of the garden. They could hear the voices in the kitchen.

"He was so forgetful!" Mum was saying loudly. "Do you remember, Dad, that time he came home in his football kit and boots after a match? And he'd already lost his plimsolls and mislaid his wellingtons somewhere, and Mum discovered that he'd left his uniform and shoes, coat, everything in school, so she sent him back to get them but it was all locked up."

"Oh, yes," cried Auntie Bird. "I remember that! Estelle was so cross. He hadn't got any shoes to wear to school in the morning, so she sent him in full kit and football boots, with a note to the teacher, to teach him a lesson. I'll never forget the look on his face!"

There was a great burst of laughter: Mum's, Dad's, Auntie Bird's and Grandad's: Grandad was laughing.

David fetched his belongings from upstairs. As he came out of the bathroom, he remembered with sudden clarity the first day that he had stood on this landing, the unfamiliar smells and sights. Now Grandad's braced trousers hanging on the back of the chair seemed as ordinary as the sight of his own trainers.

He ran down the stairs, passed the camel clock, stopped and deliberately turned into Nan's room. It was dark now, the street lights were coming on. The room *Was* different: he could feel it. Everything looked the same, but he knew something had changed. He picked up the photo that lay flat on the chest, crossed the hall to the front room and stood it on the sideboard next to one of Eric. Eric, Nan and Gordon smiled back at him.

Lizzie had fallen asleep, her head lolling onto David's shoulder. The pungent smell of onions from the boot was invading the car. No one had spoken for some while: each of them contained in their own cocoon of thoughts, as the car hummed along in the dark.

"Mum?" said David suddenly. "Did you really run away?"

"Who told you that?" asked Mum, turning her head.

"Auntie Bird. Where did you go?"

Mum took a deep breath. "I took the train to London and then rode round and round on the Underground. But a policewoman spotted me – just as well. I had nowhere to go."

"What happened then?"

"Well, I didn't want to go home. So Auntie Bird arranged for me to stay with her sister in Beckenham for a bit. I was sixteen – I'd left school, so she found me a job and later I started nursing."

"Was that how you met Dad?"

"Yes, I suppose it was. He was a student then – we met in a pub."

"*The Cat and Fiddle*," said Dad.

"It was the purple flared trousers that attracted me to him," giggled Mum.

"I never wore purple flared trousers," protested Dad.

"It's funny . . ." said David a few minutes later as he watched the cars flash past out of the darkness.

"What is?" said Dad.

"If Eric hadn't died, Mum probably wouldn't have gone to Beckenham, she wouldn't have met you and I wouldn't have been born. I wouldn't exist, would I?"

He could see Dad's eyes studying him in the rear mirror.

"No – you're probably right," he agreed and David saw a look pass between him and Mum.

"I don't know what I'm going to do with all those onions Grandad gave me," yawned Mum later.

"I'll make some onion soup," offered David.

"But you hate onions!" insisted Mum.

"Not the way Grandad cooks them," said David.

Another look travelled from Mum to Dad.

"He showed me how to slice onions so that they don't make you cry," he continued.

"Does it work?" asked Mum.

"Not every time," said David.